A Miranda Rae Mystery

MURDER
BLOOMS AT
NIGHT

A Miranda Rae Mystery

MURDER BLOOMS AT NIGHT

Donna Bjorklund

REDEMPTION
PRESS

Published by Redemption Press, PO Box 427, Enumclaw, WA 98022.
Toll Free (844) 2REDEEM (273-3336)

Redemption Press is honored to present this title in partnership with the author. The views expressed or implied in this work are those of the author. Redemption Press provides our imprint seal representing design excellence, creative content and high quality production.

This is a work of fiction. Names, characters, businesses, places, events and incidents are either the products of the author's imagination or used in a fictitious manner. Any resemblance to actual persons, living or dead, or actual events is purely coincidental.

Unless otherwise noted, all Scriptures are taken from the *Holy Bible, New International Version*, Copyright © 1973, 1978, 1984 by the International Bible Society. Used by permission of Zondervan Publishing House. The "NIV" and "New International Version" trademarks are registered in the United States Patent and Trademark Office by International Bible Society.

Scripture references marked KJV are taken from the *King James Version* of the Bible.

Scripture references marked NASB are taken from the *New American Standard Bible*, © 1960, 1963, 1968, 1971, 1972, 1973, 1975, 1977 by The Lockman Foundation. Used by permission.

Stock Photos Purchased from:
www.canstockphoto.com
www.shutterstock.com

Credit/Attribution for Print:
© Can Stock Photo Inc. / Perfect Lazybones
© Can Stock Photo Inc. /rsaraiva
© Shutterstock / Steve Collender

Designer: Brittany Osborn

ISBN 13: 978-1-68314-029-0 (Print)
        978-1-68314-031-3 (ePub)
        978-1-68314-032-0 (Mobi)
Library of Congress Catalog Card Number: 2016939007

This book is dedicated to
Aunt Ruby
who faithfully read every word written.

ACKNOWLEDGMENTS

God has revealed himself through many blessings in the course of this writing venture. At each switchback on the uphill climb I encountered the help of family, friends, and professionals.

At the beginning of the trek, Ariele Huff, a gifted teacher, encouraged me to continue when I thought I should quit. And to my writing group Barbara, Garrett, Jim, and Petra who weren't afraid to give undisguised feedback.

To Melinda, thanks for letting me bounce around ideas and for your contribution of ideas to this fictional story along with your administrative help and the many healthy, delicious lunches.

To my friend, Will, who proofread this story from the beginning.

Sandra Byrd, you are a gifted writing coach and editor. Your help in further developing my characters and plot was invaluable.

Thanks to all at Redemption Press for getting this book published.

And last, but not least, to my dogs who had to endure late meals while I was writing.

"Now to Him who is able to do far more abundantly beyond all that we ask or think, according to the power that works within us…"
—Ephesians 3:20 (NASB)

PROLOGUE

He watched as the silver Honda Civic crawled toward the small parking area; it maneuvered around the potholes but still scraped the road now and then as it drove.

He was surprised to find she'd followed directions and had arrived on time. He'd taken the precaution of choosing this particular meeting place because he was going to have to get rid of her car and then retrieve his Toyota. Most of the good hiking and easy public access were on the southeast side, so few visitors used this parking lot on the northwest side of the park. He didn't worry they might run into anyone.

The full moon enveloped her—he knew her name was Valerie—in a halo of light that reflected off of the gold cross necklace she wore. Soon she would meet this Jesus she believed in. Oh, he'd done his homework and wasn't going to make any mistakes now that he'd finally trapped her.

All of the visits he'd made to the flower department in the Kroger grocery store had helped him ingratiate himself and win her trust. He'd made sure she was alone, waiting till there were no other customers present during his visits. He'd feigned interest in her floral arrangement skills. He'd lured her with his knowledge of botany like a trout lured to a fly. He'd even invited her to take one of his classes. He enjoyed teaching, but it didn't pay enough and wasn't going to let anyone interfere with his *other* means of making the money he needed to continue living a life of free spending. He certainly wasn't going back to surviving paycheck to paycheck.

Now, he scrutinized her movements. She got out of the car and then stuffed her car keys in the zipper pocket of the fanny pack; she looked up and around.

"Good evening," the professor called smoothly and waved his arm.

"Hello." Valerie's hesitant voice wasn't quite the enthusiastic answer he was hoping for, but her startled reaction when she looked around the remote and lonely location was pleasant to him. "Where are we?" she asked. "This doesn't look like a park."

"Didn't I explain this location is the shortest way to the flowers? It's a perfect night to see the night bloomers. I chose tonight because of the full moon. I hope you brought water and a snack, it's quite a steep hike, and you'll need the extra energy." He smiled and tried to project happiness. He did, after all, like her uneasiness.

Valerie nodded and then blurted out, "You're his brother, aren't you?"

He squirmed. How much had Jarod told Valerie? Well, it hardly mattered now that he was about to eliminate any future problems.

"Yes," he simply said. "Shall we?" The professor pointed to the trail. "We shouldn't have any problem seeing the trail with the lunar lighting, and there is not a cloud in the sky. That is unusual for this time of year, but what a treat for us! With this weather, the flowers are sure to be in full bloom."

"It is a lovely night," she stiffly agreed and then started up the trail, breathing heavily early on.

"Is something wrong?" He followed close behind her. "You don't sound like your enthusiastic self."

"I think I'm coming down with something. Maybe we should do this another day." Valerie turned and tried to walk around the professor, but he stood firm, blocking her path.

"Nonsense. The flowers are only about a mile up the trail. After viewing them, you can return home in no time." After she turned back around, he firmly pressed his hand to her back and directed her up the trail.

The professor mused at his perfect plan. He had already presold her car to a less-than-reputable wrecking yard owner, a guy who didn't ask questions and wouldn't demand registration. The murder weapon would be impossible to find because it'd be something common to the wilder . . .

He was shaken out of his reverie as Valerie took off, flying up the trail, cutting into the thoughts of his perfect plan. What had shaken her? He ran, pumping hard after the long-legged blond. She was making him work. She was fast, but as she turned the bend, she lost momentum. He dashed around the same bend but lost sight of her. The professor stopped and took a deep breath. Had she turned off the trail? Was she trying to hide?

Just listen. She tired quickly for a young woman and didn't know the area. Patience.

Ahh ... there! He heard heavy breathing ahead and soundlessly progressed toward it. He saw her to the side of the trail, hands on her knees as she tried to catch her breath, and staring into the distance. He was caught up in the exquisiteness before his eyes: the bright yellow primroses, the delicately-scented night orchid, the variety of colors of the four o'clock flower, and the chocolaty scent of the chocolate flower. All were in full bloom and emitting heavenly perfumes. He'd transplanted them a few days ago. Now his plan would be complete.

"Why did you do it?" Valerie asked between gasped breaths. "I saw Jarod suffer, and it was horrible."

Cold crawled over him. She'd figured it out.

Valerie turned toward the professor, her eyes first flashing anger but quickly widening in surprise as he raised the rock in one hand and held a knife in the other. She twisted but not fast enough, and cried out, "Oh Lord, not yet!" before collapsing face down into the flowers, like a rag doll might.

CHAPTER ONE

SATURDAY, OCTOBER 19TH

10:00 PM

The full moon's light penetrated through the leafless tree limbs, awakening the trail before Miranda. She followed Jake as he brought even more light by shining his flashlight into the thickening wilderness. The pack on her back grew heavier with each step, and they'd only started hiking up the slow incline five minutes earlier. Miranda checked the time on her digital smartwatch. It was probably too soon to ask Jake if they were close to their destination.

Miranda had grown up in a small city about 45 minutes away from Stone Ridge, where she lived now. Her parents still lived in the same house in which she'd grown up. Immediately after high school, Miranda had moved to Seattle to attend the University of Washington, and she'd stayed there till she graduated with a master's degree in counseling. Then she'd been offered a position to practice in a prestigious Seattle counseling firm. During her internship there she'd dated one of the partners; after she was hired, they'd become serious enough that Miranda had thought they would marry. She'd had no intention of leaving Seattle: it had entertainment, shopping, and the man she loved. In fact, the smartwatch had been an indulgence she'd purchased to keep in touch with clients who needed her on evenings or weekends. She was only a text or e-mail away from them in the city, where coverage was excellent.

Unfortunately, the watch had also been her undoing. One of her clients had e-mailed to say she was terminating her sessions, not because she was ready to move on her own, but because the client became engaged to the man Miranda had been dating.

Heartsick, and ashamed that she'd missed the signs, Miranda had decided to start over as far away from the city as possible. She'd found Stone Ridge and began a practice that was growing, adding clientele weekly. It had kept her so busy she hadn't had the time or the desire to get involved in another relationship. But now, with Jake, she thought she might have found someone worth exploring.

"Oops," Miranda gasped as she plowed into Jake. She'd been so lost in thought she hadn't seen him stop ahead of a tangle of roots in their path! She grabbed his pack to keep from falling. He reached for her arm and a warm tingling traveled up to her shoulder. *Lord, I am not ready for another relationship. Guard my heart.* She laughed and spoke up. "Remind me why I said yes to this excursion when I'm not even a member of the Search and Rescue team? I am not in good enough shape to hike on these trails. I keep tripping over the roots."

She knew that Jake *was* a member of the Search and Rescue (SAR) team and also a volunteer EMT and fireman. He'd been working on her yard for the last three months through his company, Naturescape, trying to get it in shape. Since then, Miranda had begun to feel as comfortable with Jake as if she had known him for years. That comfort level was ironic because Jake was the opposite in many ways of the men she had dated, especially the one she'd left without a word.

"Well, it could be you came with because my persuasive powers are too much to resist." Jake chuckled, and Miranda teasingly bumped him with her shoulder, giggling like a teenager as she did.

Jake sure had a way of getting under her skin in a good way. *Be careful.* Jake was the contrary to the type of man of whom her parents approved. Jake's ruggedly handsome face was covered by a beard. His almost black hair was long, its waves tied back with a leather strip at the base of his neck, making a ponytail. Dressed for the hike, he reminded her of an outdoorsman model for one of the big sportsman stores, not the conservative corporate type that had met with her family's approval. She really shouldn't be here, but for some reason, she couldn't say no.

"It could have been your persuasive powers, but . . . " Miranda trudged on behind Jake.

"Seriously," Jake interrupted. "This Search and Rescue training has been on the schedule for a month." Jake took her hand and led her steadily up the trail. "We chose this night because of the full moon, and the night turned out to be clear as well. I want you to see how the dogs work in addition to our spending some time together." Jake continued leading them up the slope. "You know, this might be a good job for that new puppy of yours."

Miranda grinned. "That may be, but the Search and Rescue dogs I saw were hyperactive Labrador retrievers like your little puppy, Katie. My Doc is a German shepherd. He is active, but he's not over-the-top hyper. I was hoping he might be better suited to being a therapy dog and helping me at work." Miranda was breathing hard as she spoke and climbed, but kept up with Jake on the widening trail.

"German shepherds do this kind of work too; we just don't have any in our group. Your guy could be the first." Jake entwined his fingers with hers.

As he did, Miranda flinched and almost jerked her hand away from the jolt of attraction she felt, but soon calmed and even relaxed. She really shouldn't let him think she could be more than a friend to him, but what could it hurt for him to warm her hand? His stability eased the anxiety building inside her as they traveled in the dark in the middle of nowhere.

"We're almost to the cutoff for our hiding place. See that group of tall cedars ahead?" He pointed the beam of the flashlight at the trees. "We'll turn off there and wind around to find a place where we are hidden from any angle. Usually, I find fallen logs to lean up against, and then crouch low so as not to be seen when I hear the dog coming." He dropped her hand as they approached the trees and she felt a chill once more.

After passing through the trees, they slogged through dense salal and tall sword ferns and then crawled over fallen logs stacked high enough to reach up to her waist. Jake kept waving the flashlight from side to side; she supposed he was looking for the perfect hiding place. An owl hooted and Miranda jumped. She stopped when a coyote howled at the same time a gust of wind blew the last of the leaves from the alder trees toward her.

Jake turned around and slowed his pace; he seemed to realize she wasn't right behind him and allowed her to catch up.

"Why don't you hang on to my pack the rest of the way? We're moving into a thick part of the forest where it's darker." He waited until she clutched his pack before moving forward.

Jake kept the branches from slapping her in the face and helped her over the last couple of logs before declaring that they had arrived.

A sliver beam of light allowed Miranda to see a small clearing surrounded by dense brush and a couple of fallen trees. She wondered if Jake had been here before. She prayed the dog would find them quickly. She was not only physically cold but also getting cold feet concerning the wait in this "cozy" little setting. How much did she really know about Jake?

"We're here." Jake unclipped the radio from his vest. "It could be as long as an hour before they will find us so you'll probably want to put on another jacket and some gloves. I'm going to call into the base, so they know we've reached our hiding place."

Miranda swung her pack off, pulled her jacket out and rummaged through the pack to find her gloves. She watched Jake slip two folding chairs from his pack, along with his jacket. "How did you find a place like this? It seems too perfect."

"Well, actually, I've hidden here before for a different dog because it *is* perfect. Take a seat. I like to be comfortable while I wait. When we do this during the daytime hours, I read a book or work on some of my landscape architectural drawings. Now we wait until Anne's dog finds us. Speaking of which, how did you meet Anne?"

"She made me feel at ease when I attended the church service the first Sunday I arrived in town. She even invited me to sit with her family." Miranda smiled as she remembered Anne's young son leaning over his mother to shake hands and say "Howdy" to Miranda. She'd come to learn that the young man looked a lot like his dad but had the outgoing personality of his mom. Anne was one of the reasons Miranda had agreed to this training. Anne knew Jake and trusted him, but she had told Miranda that she wasn't sure what Jake believed, spiritually. Miranda had assured Anne that dating was the last thing on her mind—especially after the fiasco in Seattle. Anne also knew the other reason Miranda had moved to Stone Ridge. Miranda hadn't told anyone else.

"Anne does have a way about her that makes anyone feel relaxed in her company, as if she's known you all her life," Jake agreed. The radio crackled and both fell silent, but no voice came across the wire.

Jake whispered. "I'm not sure what that was, but we should probably be silent for a little just in case the dog is near. We want him to find us by our scent, not by our voices, during the training." He continued explaining, "Anne will use a grid, moving the dog into the wind so he can find our scent. Once the dog finds the scent, he will follow the scent cone by zigzagging toward us. When he sees us, he'll run back to Anne and bark, so she knows to follow him. He will probably run between Anne and the two of us a few times before Anne gets here."

Even in the dark, Miranda could see Jake's grin as he finished his thought. "I say he can make the trip faster and more times because he has four legs and she only has two, but Anne claims she needs to be more careful of terrain than her dog does, that's why she's delayed." Both laughed quietly.

"I'm with Anne on that count. I sure wouldn't be trying to get somewhere fast around here," Miranda whispered back.

Branches snapped, and a rustling sound came through the brush behind, causing Miranda to draw her knees up and tightly grab them. Jake's arm slipped around her shoulders, drawing her close, releasing the tension.

"What was that?" She stretched out her legs.

"Probably a deer or some other creature avoiding us. Let's keep quiet now." He withdrew his arm.

Miranda immediately missed his warmth and crossed her arms over herself instead, determined not to show any disappointment at his withdrawal. After all, she wasn't in the market for a relationship, right?

During the quiet her mind drifted to Jenny, as it often did in the dark.

Miranda had been praying about her future since the Seattle fiasco, and as she did, she had begged God's help in finding her sister, Jenny, who had deserved a future of her own. Six silent years had passed since Jenny and Valerie, Jenny's best friend, had run away. Miranda had felt responsible … and had been carrying the guilt for those long years. When Miranda had heard a rumor that Valerie had been seen near Stone Ridge, Miranda had decided to check it out. She'd hoped to find Valerie and her sister, or at least maybe Valerie, who might know where her sister was hiding.

She hadn't found Valerie but had felt at home in Stone Ridge and felt comfortable with the people she had met. She'd left Seattle for Stone Ridge, and her practice had grown.

"Penny for your thoughts," Jake whispered, his warm breath caressing her ear.

"Oh, just thinking of all the reasons I like this community. I really believe God had a part in bringing me here."

"I hope I'm one of the reasons you like this community."

She was glad it was dark because she was sure her face blended nicely with her red jacket!

"I'll have to think on that," she said before quickly changing the subject. "Have you been on any searches where someone lost has been found?"

He took the bait. "Yes, a couple. One was a woman who'd strayed from her group, and they left before realizing she was missing. We located her by calling out, and she was able to answer; unfortunately, she had broken her ankle, and we had to bring her out on a gurney. My EMT skills were pretty handy on that one. I was able to stabilize her ankle so we could transport her to the base." His voice took on an empathetic tone, showing his compassion. "The hardest one I've ever worked on was a recovery. We found an older lady, who'd wandered from her house, face down in the water of a swampy area."

Loud barking jolted Miranda out of her seat, and she almost landed in Jake's lap. He reached out and steadied her, but they both jumped when his radio crackled to life.

"Jake, we need you further up the trail—now! How fast can you get there? The dog indicated an injured woman and Anne has just radioed in the coordinates."

Miranda shooed him with arm motions, *go, go,* even though she didn't want to be left alone. He nodded to her before answering.

"It'll be a few minutes, but I'll hurry. I have to get Miranda on the trail and then I can run."

An answer came back over the radio. "Great. We'll have someone meet Miranda at the trail and take her the rest of the way."

Miranda quickly folded the chairs and put on her pack while waiting for Jake to finish talking.

"Let's go." Jake led the way toward the trail.

Miranda was glad he'd remembered to arrange for her because she would have needed the SAR team to find her if she'd been left to her own navigation. But, when they made it to the trail, no one was there to meet her. She urged Jake to run anyway.

"I'll be fine; the moon is bright enough to light the trail. If I'm careful, I won't trip on the way up. Now, go!" She pushed him on his way and then started a much slower trek.

With every noise, she shuddered. Was a mountain lion watching, or a bobcat ready to pounce, or a bear to charge? *Take a deep breath and relax. Protect me, Lord.* She needed to stop the catastrophic thinking and concentrate on the path ahead.

She soon heard a clamor of voices and noticed beams of light. Following the noise and the light, she continued to traipse up the trail. She didn't know how Jake could have run up this incline; her pack felt as if it was filled with rocks and she was breathless, even at this slow pace.

She came to a fork in the trail and didn't know which way to go. The lights seemed to be in the middle. Did they both end at the same place?

Both the overwhelming scent of pine and the tough decision on which trail to take caused her stomach to roil. *What do I do, Lord?* Peppermint came to mind. Peppermint tea had relieved her nauseous stomach more than once. She remembered having thrown some peppermint candies into her pack and rifled through it to find them. Slipping one on her tongue, she savored the sweet flavor as it slowly settled her stomach and cleared her sinuses.

All right. She could now make a rational decision and resolved to go left. That trail seemed wider which she thought meant a more heavily used trail. Starting slowly, she picked her way along it. To her relief, she found she had made the right decision—there were people approaching her from just ahead. Not wanting to be alone anymore, Miranda walked faster, almost jogging, and breathing heavily as she approached the scene.

Everyone seemed to be suspended in time, staring at Jake and the prone figure he was assessing with his gentle hand movements.

Miranda studied the figure and even from ten yards away she recognized something familiar. What was it? The long blond hair indicated that the figure was probably a woman. Miranda found herself drawn to the woman and began walking closer. As she approached the body on the ground, she noticed a metallic smell and saw blood staining the light-colored pants. There was another odor, too. More of a floral scent. Miranda looked around, but she didn't see any flowers.

Jake brushed the blond tresses away from the woman's face, and as he did, Miranda froze. A tingling originated in her hands and quickly took over her body. Miranda's past hit her full force, and she whirled, stumbling to the nearest log where she plunked down, dropping her head between her knees.

The woman on the ground was Valerie! Her sister Jenny's best friend.

CHAPTER TWO

SATURDAY, OCTOBER 19TH

11:00 PM

Miranda held her head tighter and squeezed her eyes shut, but nothing erased the vision of Valerie's battered body and blood on the ground. Miranda's nostrils were still filled with a combination of the metallic odor of blood and the mixed floral scents, causing her nausea to return. Sirens suddenly blasted, and all she wanted to do was block it out. Nothing worked.

A warm hand tentatively and slowly rubbed her back. The tension eased and Miranda slowed her breathing and then ventured a peek.

Anne, Miranda's good friend from church, had bent over her, compassion in her eyes as she gazed into Miranda's. Miranda managed a weak smile and carefully sat up, still shaking.

Her attention was immediately drawn back to Valerie. Jake was putting pressure on the wound, and someone was holding a radio near his face. She couldn't hear what was being said, but Valerie must be alive if he was working on her. Miranda desperately wanted to believe that.

"Is she … ?" Miranda grabbed Anne's arm.

"Alive?" Anne answered. "She's hanging on. They may get her out by helicopter, but the paramedics will make that call. Jake is on the

radio with them, trying to give them as much information as possible."
Anne's dog laid his head on Miranda's lap.

"Were you the one who found her?" Miranda asked as she patted the
dog's head. "Good dog." The cool dampness of the log seeped through
the double layers of clothing, bringing Miranda back to the reality of
where she was: the cold, dark wilderness. Not a place she'd have ventured
to voluntarily. Had Valerie?

"Yes, Levi found the woman instead of finding you and Jake," Anne
answered for her dog. Anne patted Miranda's back once more.

The scene seemed to have hypnotized Miranda; everyone was
moving in slow motion. The paramedics' steps were exaggerated as they
strode by and the police glided by clearing the area and starting to put
up the crime scene tape. Jake conferred with one of the paramedics, a
tall, slender woman with short, spiky, streaked hair. He stood to leave
as she took over applying pressure to Valerie. Her voice carried as she
barked orders to the others. Miranda's heart was thankful they hadn't
stopped trying to save Valerie. *Lord, let her live, and I ask you to keep
Jenny safe, too, if she's near.*

Jake stripped off the nitrile gloves as he ambled over and slumped
on the log next to Miranda. He rubbed his face. Miranda laid a gentle
hand on his arm.

"She's hanging on, but it doesn't look good. I heard them call for
an airlift." He shook his head.

Miranda had wanted to find Valerie, but not like this. She'd
hoped Valerie was still with Jenny. When the two girls had taken
off, her parents hadn't only lost a daughter, but Miranda's mom
had lost her best friend, Valerie's mom. Secretly, Miranda hoped
all parties could be reunited. She was filled with overwhelming
guilt as she remembered the night of the awful fight and then the
disappearance of the girls.

Afterward, Miranda's brother told her that Val's stepfather had put
up a "For Sale" sign shortly after the girls ran away, and that the house

sold a month later. Val's mom, Betty Anne, had never called or written Miranda's mother after the move.

Valerie had once told Jenny that her stepfather had more rules than the Bible and that he demanded obedience … or else. He'd expected his stepdaughter to comply obediently with any command.

Even now, as an adult, Miranda was not willing to cross his path and meet with his unbending disdain. "Does anyone know who the girl is?" Miranda asked hesitantly, staring at the ground, wanting someone else to identify Valerie.

"We didn't check her pockets or anything. We've been briefed to disturb as little as possible if the injuries looked suspicious. So the answer is, I don't know." Jake put his hand on Miranda's and squeezed. "Sorry you had to see this on your first hike."

"Thanks, but it's not your fault. I just hope they can identify her." The last thing she wanted was to have her name connected with Valerie's. If Val died and her stepfather, Frank, found out Miranda was there, he could take out his anger on her. She didn't know what he'd do if Val lived. Then, the truth of that last night might be revealed, and Miranda's parents would find out the truth about her. She shuddered.

The *whop whop whop* of the helicopter blades sounded as Miranda watched the medics carefully lift Valerie's body onto a stretcher and then quickly move her down the trail. The noise made conversation impossible.

Her mind wandered again to the night the girls had left; it seemed like it had happened yesterday.

"Mom and Dad are never around anymore. They're too busy with good church stuff to be bothered with me, so I can do whatever I want. Why don't you just go back to college and be a college student, Miss Perfect?" Jenny's disgusted, high-pitched voice permeated the room. "Stop telling me what I should and should not be doing."

"You have school tomorrow and talking on the phone with Valerie won't get your work done. Now, hang up and get back to your schoolwork. Mom gave me instructions to help you if needed, but also to make sure your homework gets done." Miranda took the phone away from Jenny and said goodbye to Val before slamming the handset into the cradle.

Jenny dove for Miranda. Fortunately, Miranda was bigger and stronger and, therefore, able to stop Jenny's flailing fists as Miranda almost carried her sister to her bedroom.

"I hate you and everyone in this house!" Jenny struggled to get free.

Miranda dropped her on the bed and turned to leave but caught sight of a pack of cigarettes on Jenny's desk. She picked it up, twisting around, and glared at Jenny.

"Where. Did. These. Come. From?" Miranda emphasized every word.

"They're mine. I'm old enough to buy them." Jenny grabbed at the pack, startling Miranda. Jenny stuck the pack into her back pocket.

"Give them back," Miranda's quietly menacing voice demanded.

"No!" But Jenny's voice faltered. "I can't stand it here anymore. I'm leaving."

"Go ahead, but when you need help, don't bother calling me." Exacerbated, Miranda stomped out and slammed her bedroom door before sliding to the floor in a flood of tears. When had Jenny become so sullen? Jenny wouldn't really leave home, would she? Jenny made threats all the time.

That was the last time Miranda had heard from her sister. A fresh lump landed hard in the pit of her stomach.

"Miranda?" Anne waved her hand in front of Miranda's face. "You look pale."

"Sorry, my mind was somewhere else, and I still feel a little nauseous." Miranda hadn't noticed the silence till just then. The helicopter had gone. "I have some peppermint candies in my pack; they might help." She twisted to find her pack behind her, reaching with her free hand, but it wasn't there.

"I'll get your pack." Anne pointed in the direction where a lone pack sat. "Is that it? It must have slipped off when you ran over here."

"Thanks, it looks like mine, and I'm not sure I could stand right now." Miranda felt Jake squeeze her hand, and she gave him a startled look. She'd forgotten he was sitting with her. Had he been holding her hand the whole time? He must have been.

"I have to talk to the police for a minute. Will you be okay?" Jake looked concerned.

She nodded and he and stood and let go of her hand. The cold of the night sapped away the warmth he'd offered.

Anne retrieved the pack and handed it to Miranda, who unzipped the pocket and pulled out the roll of candies. She slid one into her mouth and offered the pack to Anne. Anne took one candy, too.

"I don't know why, but the biting minty candy not only helps to settle my nausea but it also settles my thoughts." Miranda knew she needed the taste to bring her back to the present. She closed her eyes for a moment.

Save Valerie, Lord. Please let Jenny be safe too.

"Are you going to be okay, Miranda? You're still awfully pale." Anne's worried voice penetrated Miranda's thoughts.

Don't let her ask anything that forces me to reveal my relationship to the victim.

"I'll be fine, it's just a little shocking," Miranda said aloud. Then, changing the subject, she asked, "How long have you been with Search and Rescue?"

"Ah, changing the subject. Might be just the medicine you need. Levi and I have been a certified team for about three years. I've been with Search and Rescue for about six years." Anne's calming voice eased Miranda's tension.

"And Jake? How long has he been with SAR? We weren't able to talk too much before this happened," Miranda explained.

"Let's see, I think he's been with the team about three years. I didn't get to know him very well until he showed up with a two-month-old puppy, and that was six months ago. He's a great guy." Anne smiled knowingly. "I don't think I've ever seen him with a lady until I saw his interest in you. But, like I said before, I'm not sure where he stands with God."

Miranda's face heated at the implication of Jake's interest in her, and she was glad for both the cool evening and the covering darkness.

"I remember you telling me that, and after my experience in Seattle, I'm not ready to rush into anything." *Oh Lord, give me strength for wisdom and resistance in this relationship because I'm falling for Jake.* She didn't want to be humiliated again, and she didn't want to be the cause of anyone else's pain, either.

Jake came toward them, followed by one of the police officers. His badge read Deputy Sweete.

Miranda reminded herself to stay calm.

"Miranda." Jake faced her, then turned toward Anne. "Anne. This is Pete Sweete with the Stone Ridge Police Department He told me they're sending a detective from a nearby city to take charge. He'd like Anne and me to stay till the detective arrives, which means you'll have to stay too, Miranda. Will you be okay with that?" His anxious eyes met hers.

She hesitated and then in a cracked voice answered, "That should be fine, but will it be long?"

Sweete answered. "No, Miss. Detective Ryker is on his way and should be here in about a half hour." The officer turned his attention to Anne and commented, "Anne, I've heard about your dog. Did he go right up to the victim?"

"He's trained to stay a short distance away just in case anyone decides to restrain him and not let him come back to me," she answered. "So he didn't go up to the poor woman, not even when he finally brought me here. I stayed away, too. We called the base to get Jake here as soon as possible. May I go over there and let Levi run off some steam?" Anne's voice was matter-of-fact as she pointed toward a distant open area.

"Sure, but stay around so the detective can talk with you." Then Deputy Sweete looked at Miranda.

Lord, don't let him ask me anything. I don't want to lie.

"How about you, uh, Miranda is it?" he asked.

"Me what?" Miranda was confused. She hadn't been called to help with the woman.

"Did you get up close to the body?"

"Well, not close but about twenty feet away, maybe. I don't remember." Jake's arm wrapped around her shoulder.

"Pete, do you have to question Miranda? She's had a big shock and was just my guest, not a part of the official team. Can we sit over on the log until Nick gets here?" Jake's familiarity with the officer surprised Miranda.

"Well I, suppose, but don't try taking off," Deputy Sweete ordered.

"Do you know him?" Miranda asked as they walked toward the log. Jake's arm still held her close, and it felt safe.

"Yes, he's the local deputy and actually grew up here in Stone Ridge. He's a stickler for the rules." Jake looked at Miranda's red hands. "Where are your gloves?"

"In my pack. Do you know that detective Sweete mentioned, too?" She bent over the log and drew out gloves from her pack. There was something familiar about the name of that detective. Nick Ryker seemed a name she should recognize, but from where?

"Only because he is usually the one who is given assignments around here," Jake answered. "Apparently he grew up close by and knows the area. He's a good guy and will do all he can to find the person who did this." Jake pulled the chairs out of his pack once more.

"Where did they take her?" Miranda sat in the chair, grateful to be dry.

"There's a hospital nearby with a great trauma unit; it's only about an hour's drive." Jake wrapped his arm around her shoulders and drew her closer.

She felt the solid strength and warmth of the man beside her and her resolve to be friends-only quickly faded. She needed to get her mind on something else. She concentrated on the detective's name, still trying to place him. Who was he?

CHAPTER THREE

SUNDAY, OCTOBER 20TH

12:30 AM

"That's Nick." Jake bent to whisper in Miranda's ear. "I'll see if he'll take my statement first so we can get out of here. Okay?" He held her close and was reluctant to leave her. She'd been shivering spasmodically but had stopped while he rubbed her back. This wasn't how he had wanted the evening to go.

"Go ahead. The sooner I get home the better." Miranda moved away, sitting up straighter in the stadium seat. "My pup probably needs to be let out. How about your pup, Katie? She probably needs to get out, too."

"Yeah, Katie needs to get out too. I'll see how soon we can leave." Jake stood and started toward Nick, mulling things over as he walked.

What had he been thinking when he invited Miranda to the training? Nothing like this had happened before, and he'd been with the group for three years. He'd been attracted to her from the first time they met and now this. He'd noticed that her reaction to the sight of the woman on the ground was more severe than he'd seen with others in similar situations.

The spring day three months earlier when he and Miranda had first met had been perfect. The sun had shone brightly and had warmed his back as he'd stepped up to Miranda's front door. He'd knocked, and a petite woman with an inviting smile of straight white teeth had opened the door. He'd removed his work boots before entering, and as he'd followed her down the hall and right into the kitchen, he couldn't help but stare as her curly mahogany hair bounced while she talked. She was beautiful.

She hadn't given him the once-over or the, *I'm better than you*, scowl. Instead, she had made him feel as though he was the answer to all of her problems. He knew she was a counselor and had only been in town for about three months. He'd been fighting his attraction to her from that moment. Finally, he'd built up his courage to ask her to come with him on the SAR training using the excuse that the new puppy Miranda had acquired needed a job.

What does she think of me now? If there is a God—help.

Nick purposefully strode toward the crime scene, dressed in a suit, his raincoat flapping around him. He was a tall man at 6'4", wearing a serious face this evening.

"Detective," Jake called out, catching up to him. "Hi, how are you?"

Some of the detective's worry lines faded at the greeting. "Jake. Nice to see you again, but not under these circumstances. I'm doing okay, working on too little sleep and too much caffeine. I'm sorry you had to be the one to deal with this."

"Yeah, me too. This is the worst I've seen. I was wondering if you could question me first so I can get my friend Miranda home?" Jake motioned behind him with his thumb. An unexpected need to protect Miranda had overwhelmed him.

"Why don't you walk with me and let me see what's going on here, and I'll try to get to you as soon as possible. I may even be able to let you go and get your statement sometime later today." The two continued to the crime scene tape, at which Jake stopped, and Nick lifted to crouch under it. "Miranda is the name of your friend?"

"Yes," Jake answered. "Miranda Jacobsen."

"Miranda Jacobsen?" The detective looked puzzled.

"Yes. That's her name. Do you know her?" Jake couldn't hide his surprise.

"I don't really know her, but I was good friends with one of her younger sister's friends in high school. That's how I know of her." Nick stood and turned to face Jake.

Jake released a breath he hadn't known he was holding, in relief. He couldn't have been jealous, or could he have been? Jake had decided never to get married after his father had left Jake and his mother for a younger woman. That woman had been only ten years older than Jake's short life of eleven years at the time.

At church, when he was only twelve years old, Jake had heard the gossip that kids follow in their parents' sins and the teachers had even given examples showing it to be true. Jake had never wanted to hurt anyone the way his father had hurt his mom. Jake had heard his mom sob at night when she thought he was sleeping, and then she'd wake in the morning pretending nothing was wrong. He loved his mom and was determined not to put himself in a position to hurt anyone like that, ever.

The willpower he'd clung to was slowly deserting him as he became seriously attracted to Miranda. He'd called her a friend, but she was so much more than that in his mind. Could there have been a flaw in his beliefs, one which held him back from intimacy? He hoped that was true.

Jake spoke up once more. "Ah, well she was pretty shocked by the whole episode, and it'd be nice if I could take her home."

"Wait here just a minute, and I'll be right back." Nick trod toward the activity and spoke with the officers.

Jake watched Nick talk with the officers and look around the area, bending to get a closer view. A few minutes later, Nick returned.

"Jake, I have to go to the hospital, check out what's going on, and see if we know the victim's identity yet. Could you meet me there in about an hour and a half?"

"Sure, that'd give me enough time to get Miranda home. Thanks, Nick." Jake shook Nick's hand and left to get Miranda.

As he approached her, he noticed Miranda's head was bowed as in prayer. Jake touched her shoulder, and she jerked, her eyes wide with fear.

"It's okay," Jake's soothed in a gentle voice he'd used with his puppy. "I didn't mean to scare you. Nick gave us the okay to leave."

"Um, it's okay."

"It's about a mile to the truck. Are you okay with the hike?"

"Yes, I'm sure I can make it. I just want to get out of here." Miranda touched Jake's arm. "Thank you."

Jake smiled, trying not to show the worry he felt for Miranda. He wondered if there was something else going on in her mind.

Did I ever blow it! First, I bring her on a hike she wasn't too sure about, and then I leave her by herself to follow a strange trail and find me, and on top of that, she saw the brutal sight of a victim. Maybe she has every right to react the way she did. But ... still. It seems odd and over-reactive, somehow.

Miranda was wrestling to get her pack on when it was lifted from her grip. Her wobbly legs were going to have a hard time carrying her weight even without the pack, so when she saw Jake dangling it, she let him keep it.

"Thanks again. You've come to the rescue yet one more time." She took the arm Jake held out.

"You looked a little unsteady as you stood. The trail is wide enough for the two of us. It's about twenty minutes to the parking area. Hang on tight."

The trail was lit by the full moon. It was a quiet hike down and took all her concentration to stay on her feet. Jake seemed to sense her need for silence.

Finally, Jake's Dodge Ram was in view, and they picked up the pace. When they arrived, Jake opened the door and helped Miranda inside before he circled around the front and swung up into the cab and behind the wheel. He started the engine and pulled out of the parking lot. Miranda leaned against the headrest and closed her eyes, struggling to relax. The image of Valerie's battered body appeared once more, and Miranda's eyes shot open. She looked at Jake.

"Miranda, Nick said he knows you. Do you know him?" Jake asked.

It felt like his question punched her, and her breath left. "What?" She managed the single syllable. Then, a mental image from year's past flashed before her, and she remembered. Nick was the nice guy Miranda's sister, Jenny, had complained about because he was always bringing up Jesus to both Jenny and Valerie! Nick had been in the same high school class as Valerie, two years ahead of Jenny.

"Do you know Nick?" Jake asked again.

"Not really, but his name is familiar," Miranda answered cautiously. *Should I admit I know the victim? Would Jake understand? Lord, give me wisdom. Are you pushing me into this confession?*

"Nick said he was a friend of a friend of your sister, in high school. Is that right?" Jake glanced in Miranda's direction as he drove.

"Well, I'm six years older than my sister, so I was already in college when she was in high school. I remember my sister giving her opinion of a guy named Nick. But I'd never met him, not that I recall." Miranda hadn't really lied but didn't tell Jake the full extent of what she knew about Nick, either. "Are you taking me home?"

"I am taking you home, and then I'm going to meet Nick at the hospital to give my statement. He's going to see if they have identified the poor woman." Jake held tight to the steering wheel and stared straight ahead.

"Um, I should go to the hospital with you." Miranda gazed out her window, not allowing Jake to see her expression.

"Why?" Jake asked.

"I need to talk to the detective. If my suspicions are correct, he needs to know what I might know." Then to divert the anticipated next question she asked, "Can we stop by my house to let Doc out? And you'll need to pick up Katie."

Jake reached for her hand and squeezed it. "Sure, we have time, but are you recovered enough to make the trip to the hospital?"

"I should be okay. I can rest on the way. That is if you don't think you need my chatter to keep you awake."

"I'll be fine. I'm used to the calls in the middle of the night from the fire department and Search and Rescue. I wish you'd tell me what you know, though."

"Can you wait so I can see if my suspicions are right?" Miranda hung on tightly to his hand.

"Okay," Jake said and then sighed.

A few minutes later, Jake pulled the truck next to the curb in front of Miranda's home. She let go of his hand and pushed open the door before he had a chance to come around and let her out.

She tripped up the porch steps and fished her keys from her pocket. Still shaken from the whole experience, it took her a few seconds to get the door open. Jake followed her as Miranda led the way into the house. She went upstairs as Jake plodded to the kitchen, where they'd placed his pup's crate before leaving the house some hours earlier.

Doc flew down the stairs followed by Miranda, walking at a more sedate pace. She heard the backpedaling of paws on the linoleum and the telltale bang as the pup was stopped by the back door.

"Whoa, buddy. Let me get Katie and the two of you can go out together."

Miranda heard the slight squeak of the back door opening as she entered the room and watched as Jake disappeared behind the closing door.

CHAPTER FOUR

SUNDAY, OCTOBER 20TH

2:30 AM

The scent of Jake's musky cologne mixed with the sweat from his hard work filled the cab as they rumbled toward the hospital. Jake's pup Katie's head rested on Miranda's lap, breathing rhythmically in soft puffs which kept Miranda's hands warm. The steady hum of the engine should have had a calming effect, but sleep still eluded Miranda as she tried in vain to relax.

Jenny could be out there unconscious or … no, she wouldn't think about the alternative. The two girls, Jenny and Valerie, had been inseparable when they were younger, and they had left together on that fateful day six years earlier. *Were they still inseparable? I should have told Nick about Valerie. Then maybe they'd have called a search for Jenny, too. Oh Lord, what have I done?*

The secret Miranda had held in pride and guilt for so long still clung like a leech, sucking out all rational thought. If she hadn't fought and said those awful, uncaring words that night so long ago, would Jenny and Valerie have left?

Jake had graciously not pushed for her reason to go to the hospital, but how gracious would he be when he learned what she'd not said?

Miranda had been determined not to get into another relationship after the devastating blow her heart had taken. Her mother hadn't even comforted her; instead, she'd told Miranda it was God's will, and that was that. "God's will" was her mom's answer for anything that happened. Miranda supposed she was right in one respect, but just because it was true didn't lessen the hurt and betrayal she'd felt.

Miranda had never thought she'd have any attraction to another man; then she'd met Jake. He worked hard but wasn't a driven achiever. He volunteered to help, not simply to be seen by the right people. And now she was going to disappoint him with her confession to Nick. Their relationship was as good as over before it had even started.

A warm hand squeezed her shoulder, and she startled.

"Having a hard time getting to sleep? I can move Katie." Jake briefly glanced her way.

"Leave the dog, she's not bothering me and her extra body heat is helping. As tired as I am, my mind won't quit. Do you think that woman will be okay?" Miranda patted the sleeping dog's head and gazed out the side window at the passing countryside.

"I don't know. I hope so and will think positively." His voice was gentle and caring.

"I've been praying for her, and I hope she'll be okay, too." It was an opening to ask him what he believed, but Miranda didn't get a nudge from God to do so. Maybe Jake wasn't ready yet; she trusted it'd be soon. God's timing was perfect, not her timing. "How long before we get to the hospital?" she asked.

"About a half hour. Are you ready to tell me why you needed to go?"

"Not just yet." How much longer was she going to hold on to her pride? "I'll tell both you and Nick at the same time. Did you notice the flowery scent around the area? The aroma surprised me because I wasn't very close to the hurt woman. Were there some plants around her I missed?"

Jake shook his head. "I must admit, I was a little shaken at the sight of her and was concentrating on keeping her alive. I didn't notice any unusual scents or even my surroundings. We should bring that up to Nick, though."

"I thought I detected almost a hint of chocolate. Do you know of any flowers that smell like chocolate? I think I'd like you to put one of those in my garden." Miranda's head leaned on the backrest.

"I'll have to do a little research. The only one I can think of off of the top of my head is in the mint family. The scent is chocolate mint, and it smells great, but you have to rub the odor off of the petals and sniff your fingers to get the full effect—not something that emits scent for yards. It's easy to grow, and if it dies off in the winter, it will come back in the spring. It's almost like a weed, but it spreads a little slower. Do you think you'd like some of that? I can also look into other plants, too." His voice seemed to fade.

The next thing she knew, Miranda felt her body shaking, but she felt in a dream state. Were they on a dirt road? Her hands felt hot and trapped.

"Miranda."

She heard her name through a haze and slowly her eyes drifted open. Her head fell forward, and she saw Katie had repositioned half her body on her lap. No wonder her hands were hot, and she couldn't move them. Miranda gazed up at a smiling Jake, who had been shaking her.

"I guess I fell asleep. We must be at the hospital."

"Yep." Jake nodded. "Wait there, I'll get your door."

"Hey, Katie girl, you need to get up." The pup stretched and lifted her head to stare at Miranda. Miranda smiled and helped Katie move into Jake's vacated seat. She watched as the dog curled in the seat and went back to sleep.

Jake opened Miranda's door and helped her out.

"Are you sure you want to come in now? Couldn't what you have to say wait until tomorrow?"

Miranda shook her head, and they started toward the emergency entrance. As soon as they were through the doors, she was overwhelmed by the competing odors of antiseptics, heavy perfumes, sour vomit, and sweat. Her stomach roiled. She had to stand strong, but even taking a deep breath wouldn't help manage the chaos around her. Most of the chairs around the perimeter of the room were occupied, and the rows in the middle of the expansive room were filled. She found an empty chair and sat in it.

A weeping woman stood in the embrace of a man—her husband, maybe—and a young lady in a wheelchair sat nearby, her knee wrapped in an ice pack. A mother held a towel around an ice pack pressed against her son's bleeding nose; she tried to hold him still while he screamed in pain. There were others too. Miranda noticed a couple of people holding towels on cuts, blood seeping through the cloth, and a forlorn teen holding her jaw and trying to turn away from the crowd so no one could notice her bruised face. So many sat in the waiting room still needing help. The soft murmuring was almost a roar in her ears.

Lord, be with each one here, giving strength and comfort. Miranda's tender heart shone forth in the tears about to overflow and slip down her cheeks. She swiped them with her hand then closed her eyes and swallowed hard.

When she opened her eyes again, Jake had made his way too and had already started speaking with Nick, near the double doors to the emergency rooms. The check-in counter had a line four deep, and Miranda wove her way around the seats and the people in line toward the men. She needed to tell Nick what she knew before she lost her courage.

"Ahh, here she is." Jake laid his arm around her shoulders, and she leaned into him, gathering her strength, even if this might be the last time she could lean on him.

"Miranda." Nick gave a slight nod in acknowledgment. "What do you need to say?"

"Nick, I'm pretty sure I know the victim."

Both men stared in astonishment. Miranda swiveled her head to move her gaze back and forth between the two men and then nodded as her face heated.

"Yes, and I should have said something when I saw you earlier. My only excuse is that I didn't want to become involved. Can you keep my name out of this?" She wanted to know if she could avoid Val's stepfather's wrath. All those years ago he had threatened her. She'd never told anyone. She wasn't even sure why he'd threatened her or if he could follow through, or even if she was the only one he'd threatened.

"It depends on where the investigation goes, Miranda. I'll try to keep your name anonymous, but I can't promise," Nick countered.

"Okay. I need to tell you anyway. The woman is named Valerie Buchanan. I believe she was in your class in high school, and she was my sister Jenny's best friend." Miranda explained.

Jake stiffened.

"Ah yes, yes, she was," Nick stuttered.

"I'm sorry, but I had to tell you now. Remember how inseparable the two girls were?"

Nick nodded.

"I'm wondering if Jenny, my sister, is out there, too?" Miranda covered her face with her hands, no longer able to hold in the tears. Jake turned her in his arms and held her tight. *Maybe he doesn't hate me yet. Lord, help.*

She was still alive! How could he have been mistaken, believing that the dead weight he'd carried almost half a mile to it's supposed final resting place wasn't truly dead at all? How could he have known the Search and Rescue teams were out practicing?

He couldn't have.

The crack of her skull had cinched it for him. Who could live in spite of a cracked skull and a knife wound that was bleeding heavily? No one.

He was new at this. His stepbrother's death hadn't really counted as murder, even though he had provided the spiked drugs that had sent Jarod into an overdose coma from which he never recovered.

I need to think.

Okay, the professor knew quite a few people who worked at the hospital because he was a regular visitor, pretending to visit an older relative, but instead collecting his payment in prescription narcotics for supplying the drug of choice for a few choice employees. He'd simply borrow one of the employees' ID badges and grab some scrubs, then he could finish her off. He'd add a little something to her IV drip to send her into a deep sleep … with no chance of recovery.

Now that he had his plan in place, the professor needed to concentrate on getting to the cars before the police did. He needed to keep quiet for a little while longer, making sure the police stayed close and didn't start wandering off to find things he didn't want them to find.

Luckily, he'd stayed hidden and heard the commotion, or else he would never have known the job wasn't complete. He didn't read newspapers. Unless the situation was reported on TV, he'd have remained ignorant of Valerie's status.

His muscles were getting stiff. Maybe he'd try to get to the cars; the officers weren't moving far from the scene. The girl's car was old enough that he could put it in neutral and let it roll, silently, for a while.

Covered in darkness, he slowly rose and located an animal trail he knew led in the opposite direction of all the current activity. He didn't live in this too-small town anymore but was glad that he'd played in this wilderness area as a boy and could still remember all the back trails. They were a little overgrown, but still there.

He pulled out Valerie's car key and put the transmission in neutral before letting it roll with only a slight push from him.

He was home free.

CHAPTER FIVE

SUNDAY, OCTOBER 20TH

5:00 AM

There was a strained silence between them on the ride back to Miranda's house, silent of course, but for the soft snoring of the dog. She wasn't sure what to say. She'd compartmentalized the past so successfully and had hidden it so well that, now that it was out in the open, Miranda was stung with a loss for words.

The truck drew up to her house; Jake left the engine running as she turned to release the door latch and then swiveled her head toward him before speaking.

"Would you like to come in for some coffee? I'd like to explain a little more about Jenny and Valerie."

"Miranda, you don't have … "

"I know," she interrupted, pleading, as she met his confused gaze. "But I'd like to, and you deserve that much."

"There's a debriefing meeting this afternoon, and I have to get some sleep before attending. You should come, too. The meetings do help."

"This won't take long. I think I'll pass on the meeting, though." Miranda opened her door, stepped out of the truck, and then shut the door before shuffling toward the house. As she rummaged for her keys, she heard another door slam and saw a little black shadow cross her path. He was coming in to hear her out. *Thank you.*

They entered her home, and Katie's ears perked at the sound of the whining coming from upstairs.

"Coming, Doc." Miranda tromped up the steps to let her dog out. "Go on into the kitchen, Jake. Oh well, you know the routine. Watch out for the Tasmanian devil on his way!" Doc rocketed down the stairs, barely touching the steps as he flew down the hall, making it to the landing before Miranda had even made it halfway down the stairs. "Thanks for letting him out," she said, watching as Jake checked out the flowers on the table.

"I see you still have the flowers I cut from your garden," he said. "I didn't notice them earlier."

The bright purple, orange, yellow, and white blooms filled a vase set in the middle of the kitchen table, casting a subtle, sweet fragrance throughout the house.

"They seem to be doing well. Would you like coffee or tea?" Miranda got to the kitchen and then filled the teakettle with water and the coffee pot carafe.

"I'll have tea. Do you have a chamomile blend?"

"Yep. Have a seat. I think the dogs will be okay for a few minutes." Miranda flicked the switch on the electric teakettle. It didn't take long for the water to boil and then she filled two mugs with the boiling water, dropping in the tea bags.

The sweet scent of the natural honey flavor mixed with the light chamomile aroma. She preferred her tea without any cream or sugar, but both were available for Jake. He stirred in a little sugar. Miranda blew on the steaming brew to cool it enough to drink, and then sipped the tasty drink before taking in a deep breath and speaking.

"Well, as you know, my sister Jenny and her best friend Valerie had taken off about six years ago." She held her mug with both hands and took in a deep whiff of the calming tea before continuing. "I have been making discreet inquiries to learn if anyone has seen my sister the last couple of years." She paused for a moment and then continued.

"Jenny was only sixteen when she took off with Valerie. My parents had the police looking for her until she turned eighteen, but somehow both girls were able to evade the officers. Jen was an angry teen and particularly angry the night she left with Valerie."

Miranda wasn't ready to reveal her part in causing the teen's rising temper that night.

"The next morning, Valerie's parents stormed into our house yelling we were to blame. Well, in truth, Valerie's stepfather did most of the yelling. My mom and Valerie's mother were both in tears. My calm, steadfast dad blanched with each accusation Frank fired at them." Miranda set the mug on the table still holding it with both hands looking into its depths to gain courage.

"My mom and dad continued to go to church, but Mom mentioned to me that shortly after the disappearance, Frank and Betty Anne, Val's parents, stopped attending services. My mom had tried calling Betty Anne several times but never received a call back. Then, about four months later with no word from the teens, my dad saw a "For Sale" sign in front of Val's parents' home. The house sold fast, and they were gone."

She'd leave out the part when Frank called to threaten her if he ever found out she knew where Val was but didn't alert him. Of course, she hadn't known where Val was … until now. Would he still carry out his threat if he knew she'd merely heard Val was in the vicinity but had said nothing?

"Miranda, I'm sorry." Jake leaned over the table and placed his hands over hers. "Why did you come here to Stone Ridge?"

Oh no, Jake is too perceptive, almost as though he could read my mind. Miranda hesitated, then sighed.

"You are too astute." She grinned. "I'd heard from a friend, who'd heard from an acquaintance, that Valerie had been seen in one of the major grocery chains here though I never actually saw her before tonight. But I was ready for a change from the big city and had grown up not too far from here, so I considered it for myself, too." She wasn't about to reveal her horrible breakup in Seattle. "The town is close enough to my parents so I can visit for an evening, yet far enough away to live my own life. And surprisingly for a non-outdoors girl, I feel at home," she admitted with a half-smile. "How about you? I realize you are an outdoors guy, but was there some other reason you picked this area?"

A moment of silence ticked by. "I will tell you all about it but at another time. I think we both need some sleep. Are you sure you won't go to the meeting this afternoon?" Jake rose from his chair.

"I'm sure." She stood and, after bringing the dogs in, Miranda followed Jake to the door.

Jake turned and wrapped Miranda in a hug. She leaned into his strong chest and breathed in that outdoors scent unique to Jake. He gently released her and walked out of the house. She leaned against the doorframe holding Doc's collar and waved as the truck took off.

Maybe we're still okay. Lord, guard my heart if he's not the man for me.

Miranda locked the door and then heaved herself up the stairs. After locking Doc in his crate, she plopped into bed, not bothering to change clothes. Sleep was fitful with vivid dreams of the two teens: one a freshmen and the other a junior, both dressed in formal wear. The younger girl wore a light sage gown, showing off her russet curls, and the older wore a fuchsia full-skirted gown, showing off her long, blond tresses. Neither had a date, but they were gaily jabbering away in the backseat of the car as Miranda drove them to the school.

In her dream, Miranda jolted at the yelling, and then she was yelling back at her sister. The noise wouldn't stop; she tried covering her ears, but it didn't help.

Slowly, Miranda recognized the noise was Doc's barking and began to wake up. She whisked the covers off of herself and sat up. The clock shone 3:00. "Oh Doc, I'm sorry." Miranda let him out in the backyard. The phone rang. "Hello?"

"Miranda, where have you been? I've been trying to call you all morning."

"Hi, Mom. I had a late night, and I've been sleeping. Actually, I just got up. Is dinner still at six tonight?"

"Yes. Will you be able to make it?"

Miranda wanted to roll her eyes; she'd never missed except when the cheating boyfriend had insisted she go out with him instead. "Of course, I'll be there. Did you need me to pick up anything on the way?"

"Yes, I forgot the asparagus, and we're almost out of butter. What were you doing up so late last night?"

"I'll tell you when I see you. Is it okay to bring Doc?" Her mom never missed a detail and would want to know everything. If she could, her mom would know about things before they even happened.

"Sure, bring Doc. See you soon. Love you."

"Love you too, Mom."

Miranda let Doc in and then went up to shower. As she stepped out of the shower, her phone rang again. They'd have to wait a few minutes, and then she'd call them back. Her invigorating mint soap helped her to feel both clean and awake, refreshing her senses and clearing her mind. She knew she'd better hurry if she was going to both stop by the store and make it to her parents' house on time.

She picked up the phone; caller ID showed Jake's name. She'd call him from the car on her Bluetooth. Leashing Doc, she opened the door but had to stop him from pulling so she could lock the door behind him. Leash manners, that's what he needed. She had signed up for obedience sessions, but the classes were full until November. The lock finally clicked, and the dog dragged her out through the rain and to her car. She really should get in the habit of parking in the garage; then, at least, her hair might be more manageable. Instead, she dealt with frizzy curls.

Using voice control, she called Jake.

"Hello?"

"Hi, Jake. I haven't listened to your message yet. What's going on?"

"Miranda, it sounds like you're driving."

"I'm on my way to my parents' for dinner. How did the meeting go?"

"It was good. Nick stopped by and asked for our help."

She was silent for a moment and then asked, "How?" Out of the corner of her eye, she could see Doc cocking his head from side to side when he heard Jake speak but couldn't see him.

"Nick wants volunteers to go out in pairs on the trails and let him know if we find anything suspicious. He doesn't have enough officers to cover all the ground." He hesitated then blurted, "I volunteered you as my partner. We could bring the dogs and have a nice leisurely hike. How about it?"

Miranda pulled into the parking lot before answering. "I just drove into the Kroger grocery parking lot and have to get some things for my mother. Can I call you on my way home? I have to think about it for a bit." She wasn't so sure she wanted to go out on the trails again so soon.

"Okay. I'll talk with you later."

Miranda pushed the end button, dropping her forehead to the steering wheel. Lifting her head, she opened the windows slightly for Doc and then went into the store. She walked into the sweet aroma of cinnamon rolls, brownies, and cookies. Her mouth watered, but as tempting as it would be to buy something, she resisted, knowing her mother would serve some gourmet dessert after dinner. The store was crowded, and as she waited in the checkout line, she spotted the floral department.

Jake had been after her to get some plants for her office, to make the environment feel less sterile. She'd thought the artwork she'd picked out would have done that, but a nice plant or two might help. She had just the spots for them, too. After paying for the groceries, she made her way to the flowers and knelt to look at a couple of Christmas cactuses and the orchids. Orchids might take too much work. She'd stick with easier plants.

A woman's voice spoke up. "You knew Valerie."

Was she speaking to her? Miranda didn't think so. She stiffened in her crouched position, not wanting to be noticed. She wasn't in the habit of listening to other people's conversations, but Valerie's name had piqued her interest. It was probably another Valerie, not her Valerie, the Valerie in the hospital.

"No, I don't think so," the man replied.

"Sure, I saw you talk with her a few times. Aren't you the professor at the university extension in town?"

"I am, but there are other professors too. Maybe I look like one of them."

Curious, Miranda tilted her head enough to see a tall man with a crew cut. When he turned to the side somewhat nervously, she noticed he had a goatee.

"Val told me she was excited about seeing some flowers that bloomed at night and she was going to take one of your classes. She signed up for one next quarter. I hope she can still make it, and that everything is all right. I'm here because she didn't show up for work today, which is unusual."

Miranda started trembling, and an uneasy feeling started in her stomach. This had to be her Valerie they were talking about. Did this professor know Val or not?

"I'm sorry, but I think you have the wrong professor." He turned to leave, but the woman didn't stop talking.

"Well, she encouraged me to see those night blooming plants, too, so she gave me the directions she was given. I thought I'd bring a friend and go see them. Have a nice evening."

Miranda was frozen in place. *Lord, what does this mean? What am I supposed to do?* She watched from her stooped position as the professor left. He stopped walking, turned around, and his gaze somehow found hers and their eyes locked briefly. A tingling went straight up her spine.

CHAPTER SIX

SUNDAY, OCTOBER 20TH

EVENING

Lightheaded and wobbly, Miranda swayed for a moment before catching her balance.

"Are you alright ma'am?" The clerk who had just been speaking to the professor now spoke to Miranda.

No, I am not. Take a deep breath. Oh Lord, please stop my head from spinning. I need to do something and talking with the clerk seems the first step. I won't sit by and do nothing anymore.

"I ... I think I'll be okay. Standing up so fast wasn't the smartest move." Miranda picked up a Christmas cactus and brought it to the counter. "I was looking for a couple of plants for my office. Do you have any recommendations? I need something that doesn't need a lot of attention, and I thought about this one."

"Sure. You might also try philodendrons and if you like something with a flower, a peace lily. Both are easy; in fact, if you forget to water them for a time they'll come back to life when you remember to give them some. The Christmas cactus you have there takes more care." The clerk moved around the counter and led Miranda to the plants she'd been speaking of. "Another thing about the peace lily, it's supposed to clean the air in the room in which it's placed."

"I like that idea. I'll take one of each and a Christmas cactus for my receptionist. She has a green thumb even if I don't." Miranda wanted to ask about Valerie. *Ask now.* "Um, I couldn't help overhearing your conversation earlier. Did you know that clerk named Valerie very well?"

"Not really, but we'd work together once in a while. She'd moved here only about six months ago."

"Did she move here with a friend?" Miranda felt a thread of hope that she might be close to finding Jenny.

"I'm not sure, but I know she told me she had a roommate."

"Did you ever see her roommate?" Miranda asked.

"No," the clerk replied.

"How long had Valerie worked here?" Miranda changed the subject and stuffed her trembling hands in her coat pocket. How could she find out about Val's roommate?

"Only about four months but Val had a gift for putting together stunning bouquets, and she definitely had a green thumb. I think she was going to get a degree in botany. When the botany professor encouraged her to sign up for his class, she was so excited she talked nonstop about it." The clerk carefully set each plant in individual bags.

"I overheard something about flowers that bloom at night?"

"Oh yeah. That was another subject she chattered on about. She said she was going to see those flowers. She didn't say when she was going, but I talked her into telling me where they were supposed to be. I have a friend who wants to go with me another time." The clerk scanned the prices.

"Do you know that man you were talking to earlier?" Miranda bent her head to scrounge in her purse and find her billfold. She didn't want to let the clerk see her eagerness.

"I don't know him specifically, but he sure looked like the guy Valerie talked with while she was working. I happened to be in the store and saw them talking a couple of times. But he should know—and he said it wasn't him when I asked." The young woman chattered away. "After all there, is more than one botany professor at the college."

"Did you know Valerie's last name?" Miranda was worried the woman might think she asked too many questions, but she needed to know if it was the same Valerie as the woman in the hospital. But Valerie might well have married and now have a different last name.

"No, we didn't know each other very well." The clerk didn't seem to be bothered by all the questions.

"Thanks." Miranda swiped her card and keyed in the information. Then she slipped the debit card back into her purse. She wanted to know where the night-blooming flowers were, and maybe this young lady could help her. She tugged out a business card and then asked, "Would you call me if you locate the flowers? I'm curious, too."

"Sure." The clerk accepted the card and slipped it in her pocket.

Miranda picked up her bags and left the store. It was a wonder she hadn't seen or heard about Valerie in Stone Ridge, but she did not shop at this store very often.

Her parents hadn't mentioned anything about Val, so they must not have known she was in town either; her mother was a Safeway shopper. In the car, Miranda wondered if she should tell her mother what had happened to Valerie or just keep her mouth shut. How would her mother take the news? What if she went to the hospital only to be ignored by Valerie's parents? Or, could there be a reconciliation? Would the clerk call her about the night blooms? Too many questions with no answers. *Lord, please give me wisdom.*

A little later, she arrived at her parents' home. "Mom, Dad, where are you?" Miranda burst into the house with Doc in the lead. She moved into a kitchen filled with the rich aroma of the roast and potatoes baking in the oven. "Mmm, it smells good in here." Doc went to the oven, gave an appreciative sniff, and then pawed at it. "Off!" Miranda commanded the dog. "It's time for you to go outside in the back." She let him out the door as her mother walked into the room with open arms.

"Sweetheart, it's good to see you. How is work?" Harriet released her daughter.

"Good to see you, too, Mom. Work is going fine. I add a couple of new clients weekly. At this rate, my schedule will be as full as I can handle within a month." Miranda smiled and then asked, "Can I help?" She handed the asparagus and the butter to her mom. *Well, Lord, I haven't heard from you. What does that mean?* She'd see where the conversation went and then decide. If nothing was said or asked about Valerie, Miranda wouldn't volunteer any information.

Dinner was delicious. The moist meat fell apart, melting in her mouth, and the potatoes were done to perfection: a little crispy outside but soft on the inside. The asparagus was tender.

"Mom, that was delicious. I haven't had such a nice meal since last week. Oh, and where's Robert?" Miranda's brother usually came to Sunday evening meals too but lately had excuses, usually work related.

"He had a project to finish and it's close to the deadline. He called yesterday to tell us. Now, tell me why you were sleeping all afternoon." Harriet started to clear the table.

Of course he did. I need to call Robert and find out why he seems to be avoiding the family Sunday meals.

"I went on a Search and Rescue training last night. A friend thought I should go to see if it was something I might be interested in training Doc, to give him a release of all his pent-up energy. It ran pretty late." She hadn't gotten the nudge from God, so she kept silent concerning Valerie. Her mom surprised her by not saying anything else.

After dessert, Miranda helped with the dishes and then collected Doc to leave. She hugged both her parents and drove home. She'd decided her parents had a right to know about Valerie, but not before the police located and notified Valerie's parents. Bringing up the past could only surface the hurt they had so successfully hidden beneath their daily facades. She knew Jenny was never far from any of their thoughts. Even so, Miranda felt guilty about her silence.

Miranda called Jake and affirmed her decision to go on the hike tomorrow night. Driving past the grocery store reminded her of the clerk. *Will she call me before Jake and I leave for our hike tomorrow night?*

CHAPTER SEVEN

MONDAY, OCTOBER 21ST

EVENING

Miranda pushed open the car door, jumped out, and slammed her door shut before opening the back car door and grabbing Doc's leash. They both rushed to get into the house. After letting Doc out to the backyard, she ran upstairs to get ready for the hike.

Work had been taxing with one new client and, as it happened, that had been the last appointment of the day. The client had seemed defeated and had reasons for why any of the suggestions Miranda had proposed would fail. So Miranda had spent extra time after the client left mapping out a plan for the next visit. At least she was able to talk the client into coming back. But now Miranda was running behind schedule.

She'd have to change from city counselor to outdoors hiker in a matter of the few minutes before Jake arrived. She left her coat over the railing and threw her shoes off in the hallway on her way to her room. Fortunately, she had her hiking clothes on the bed. She was organized and usually neat, but it'd take too much time to hang anything up just then, so her suit dropped on the floor where she stood and remained there. She slipped into layers of synthetic thermal tops to keep her warm and dry and pulled on merino wool leggings under nylon hiking pants.

As she finished taming her hair into a band, the doorbell rang. She took a look in the mirror and—for a rush job—her hair was surprisingly captured and not fly-away. She heard Doc barking in the backyard as she took the stairs two at a time down to answer the door. She straightened up and then held her breathing to a normal pace before opening the door to see Jake's fist ready to knock.

She was unprepared for the current surging through her as she focused on Jake's warm brown eyes, and she stepped back from him at the power of it. There seemed to be magnetism between them. She held his gaze and noticed the gold flecks which sparkled in those brown eyes as he offered a crooked smile. Most of his face was hidden behind the neatly trimmed beard. She had always thought men were trying to hide something behind their beards or were too lazy to shave, but Jake's beard was part of him. When he moved forward and bent toward her ear, the tickle of the bristles sent tingles all over her.

"Are you ready?" he asked softly.

"Um, almost." She struggled to answer and drew back a little further so she could think straight. "Doc is in the backyard, and my pack is ready. Just need to grab my flashlight. Have you had dinner? I haven't eaten yet. Do we have time for me to make a sandwich?" She babbled her thoughts aloud, trying to regain her equilibrium.

"I have eaten. Go ahead and make a sandwich and I'll get Doc into the truck with Katie." Jake followed Miranda down the hall to the kitchen.

Miranda slid her sandwich in a resealable bag, grabbed her flashlight and pack, and then hastened out the door. Jake was waiting to open the truck door for her and then circled around the front and slipped in behind the wheel.

"How was your day?" Miranda asked as she buckled her seatbelt.

"It was uneventful and dry. Dry is pretty important when you work outside." Jake grinned and pulled the truck away from the curb. "How was your day?"

"It was good, but the last appointment went longer than normal. I rushed home, and that's why I didn't get dinner." Miranda took a bite of the sandwich. "Have you done a lot of hiking?"

"Actually, yes. My mom loved hiking, and she would take any opportunity she could to bring me along. It was a low-cost activity. I also joined Boy Scouts and learned a lot about camping. But once during one of the Scout outings, we were supposed to go get branches for a fire. We were going to roast hot dogs and marshmallows. But I, being the expert in my own eyes because my mom and I had done so much hiking, thought I could go further to get more wood and still find my way back." Jake glanced at Miranda. "Yeah, you probably guessed. I got lost and panicked. Well, after some time had passed I heard whistles blowing and remembered I had a whistle, too. So I blew for all I was worth and they found me. After all that I was pretty sure we'd have to hike for an hour to get back, but I was actually less than a quarter mile from the campsite."

Miranda giggled.

"You laugh, but I can tell you it was serious business."

"Oh Jake, I picture a miniature of you in a blue shirt with all the badges and a yellow bandana around your neck, moving like a bumper car." Miranda put her hand over her mouth to cover the laugh burbling up. "And I can see your cheeks filled while you're blowing the whistle." Miranda laid her hand on his bicep. He pursed his lips together trying not to laugh, but when he glimpsed at her, they both broke out in laughter.

"Okay, it really wasn't that funny," Jake said. The dogs wanted to join in and poked their heads over the seat, trying to lick faces. "Katie get back." Both dogs retreated into the back seat at the sound of Jake's voice.

"Any other hiking stories?"

"Oh, I see what you want. You want to hear about when I got in trouble. I'm on to you!"

"Well, yes. It's a lot more entertaining than my journeys through the city streets," she admitted.

"You really haven't been hiking before, and you lived close to all of this wilderness?"

"Well, after hearing what's happened to you, I'm glad I haven't done any hiking. I'm a jogger. My parents weren't involved in any sports. My brother, sister and I learned all we know about athletics from school."

"I don't have any other youth stories like the Boy Scout experience because my mom was always prepared. She taught me the essentials, and we always had backpacks with plenty of water and food. She used well-traveled trails and had a compass. Mom was amazing. She wonders to this day why I'm living out here building a business from the ground having left a well-paying, secure job as a landscape architect. I keep telling her it's because of all the hiking we did together. Then mom rolls her eyes as if I've lost my mind."

"She sounds like a great mom. Do you visit your parents often?" Miranda hadn't heard anything about Jake's dad and wondered why.

"I don't see my mom very often. My dad left us." Jake focused on the road; his voice was a monotone talking about his dad.

Miranda changed the subject, trying to get the easygoing camaraderie back. "What kind of experiences have you had with Search and Rescue?"

"Once I was following a dog team and the dog found a group of campers. It was 2:00 a.m., and the dog was barking up a storm. The campers weren't too happy with us. And, once I started my hike too late and ended up staying the night." Jake slowly shook his head. "Fortunately, it wasn't too cold, and it didn't rain. I found some big rocks for a shelter and used some cedar tree branches as a roof. The ground was fairly soft, but I still didn't sleep well."

"Jake! How did you know where it was safe to stay? Did you find your way back in the morning?" Miranda clenched her fists. After seeing Valerie's body, she wondered if it could be safe out there for anyone.

"It's as safe out there as sleeping under the stars in your backyard. You get the same wildlife visitors."

"You're kidding."

"Yeah, there's probably more wildlife in your backyard," Jake answered with a grin, and Miranda soft-punched him. "Ouch. And just so you know, yes, I did make it back to my truck in the morning." He smiled crookedly once more, then continued, "You just have to find a place like a crevice between large rocks to protect you from the weather." The truck slowed, and Jake turned into the parking lot. "We're here. Wait there and let me be a gentleman." After shutting off the car, Jake circled and opened Miranda's door, helping her out. Then he let the boisterous pups out, holding both leashes. "We've been given a small area with a short, steep hike to cover." He handed Doc's leash to Miranda.

"I'll follow you," she said.

Flashlights shining, they started up the trail. Jake had seemed perfectly happy until the mention of his father. Miranda wondered what had happened in his family, and what secrets Jake was holding back. She didn't want to upset the hike by asking, though. Besides which, she was on a mission to see if her sister might be out here. She started waving her light from side to side, scanning the trail ahead.

"Jake, what kinds of signs would we see if someone had left the trail to hide maybe?" Her flashlight hovered on a tree; it seemed as if the bark had been peeled away. Before he could answer, she spoke up. "What happened to this tree?" Jake added his beam to hers.

"That's a madrona; the bark sometimes peels away." Jake started up the trail again. "If someone did leave the trail, we might see crushed leaves in a footprint shape, or we might get lucky enough to see trampled ferns or bushes, or even a piece of cloth ripped from their clothes caught on brambles."

"How easy would it be to hide your trail?" Maybe her sister could hide without anyone seeing any evidence.

"I've never had to worry about that, but I suppose it wouldn't be too hard. If it's dark and you're not being sought by an experienced tracker, a person could probably easily hide the tracks. We probably won't find anyone tonight. We're mostly just around to keep up an appearance of activity out here."

Jake may not be looking for anyone, but Miranda wanted to be sure her sister wasn't out here. The quiet was undisturbed except for their footsteps and an owl's hoot now and then. The moon was still almost full and shone a halo of light around them.

"I still remember the scent of flowers on Valerie," Miranda said, following close behind him. "Are there any wildflowers here with a strong fragrance?"

"I plant a lot of scented flowers in gardens, but I don't see too many out on the trails. Are you sure she wasn't wearing a perfume of some kind?" Jake asked.

"I suppose it's possible, but for as many different perfumes as I've come across, nothing has even been similar. I wouldn't choose to put on a chocolate-scented cologne!"

"Why, do you think someone would want to lick it off?" Jake chuckled.

"Ha-ha. Funny guy." Miranda smiled but did not stop waving her light carefully on each side of the trail.

Jake suddenly stopped, and Miranda slammed into him as Doc surged past them both. Miranda started to tremble and felt the blood drain from her face. *Lord, what's wrong? I can't faint—please hold me up!*

Miranda started her deep breathing exercises to calm herself and as she did, she caught a familiar scent. Those flowers. What was going on? "Jake, what's wrong?" Something dark pierced her being. She wanted to flee, but clung to Jake's pack instead, her knuckles turning white with the effort to stay upright. She'd let go of Doc's leash, and he was, surprisingly, leaning on her.

"You remember when you asked about covering up tracks? I think someone has been here and was trying to cover up something." He trudged a couple of steps closer, dragging her with him.

"Wh ... what is it, um, you see?" The chocolate scent enveloped her, and she didn't know if she could stand much longer. "Jake, can you smell it?"

"Yes, you were right, but none of the flowers are here. Someone tried to make a fresh patch of dirt look like it's been out here forever. See how square the patch is and the random roots sticking up. Fresh." Jake turned so quickly Miranda dropped her hold on his pack. "Miranda, are you okay?" He reached to catch her and when he did, cradled her face in his warm, calloused hands. "Sit down and have a drink of water." He snagged a bottle of water from his pack and handed it to her after she sat.

"I … I need a few minutes. Something is wrong here, Jake." She didn't care if she sounded crazy.

"I agree, but you need to take it easy. Will you be okay with Doc to protect you? I need to look around and report all of this to Nick." Jake squeezed her shoulders and gazed into her eyes.

"I'm okay now. I'm going to help you." She started to get up, but the pressure of his hands kept her in place.

"Miranda, you need to stay here. I won't go too far away." He removed his hands from her and walked away, starting to search.

As soon as he was out of sight, Miranda rose slowly, wobbled a little, and then with Doc in tow, she turned opposite from the direction Jake had taken. For what was she searching? She didn't know.

CHAPTER EIGHT

MONDAY, OCTOBER 21ST

NIGHTTIME

Wading through the salal, carefully picking his way through the ferns and brambles Jake meticulously searched for any disturbance. He wasn't sure what he was looking for, but from Miranda's description of the fragrance, he'd look for some flowers strewn around the area. He was sure someone had tried to cover up something in the patch of dirt he'd just left.

He recognized the activity because he'd had to do the same thing after planting flowers for a client who then changed her mind. He'd pull out the plants and dress the area to make it look like nothing had been planted or disturbed. The similarity of this patch to his own operations was uncanny. Someone who knew what they were doing had done it, but he couldn't think of a landscape competitor in this small town.

Miranda's reaction had been almost the same as the one she'd had on Saturday night. Jake suspected there was more to the situation than what she'd already told him. He'd hoped this could have been a nice hike, and that once they reached the end of the trail, Miranda would see why he'd picked this particular area to search. At the end of the trail, the sky opened up to an incredible view of the moon and stars.

Jake couldn't believe the deep and unexpected need he had to protect Miranda. He knew she was fearful of the wilderness, and yet she asked pertinent questions, and then decided to come out again and at night.

Then it hit him. He had left her alone! What had he been thinking? Well, she had her dog with her but … he needed to get back to her. Now! What was she going to think of him? And yet, did it matter? His attraction for her was growing—but he needed to stop it. He wasn't going to be the cause of her deep heartache; because history repeats itself, he assumed he'd repeat his father's rejection of wife and family eventually too.

He'd returned to Miranda's now unoccupied location. Doc was nowhere to be seen, either. Where had they gone? "Miranda, where are you?"

"Jake." He barely heard his whispered name.

"Miranda!" He shouted. Then stood still, straining to hear more and so locate her position.

"I'm here," she called, and as he looked around, he saw her beam moving. Her voice was still barely audible, so she must have trekked a distance. Jake moved quickly in the direction of her light. She could be hurt. He'd have to warn her of the dangers of the wildlife. He was already showing how unreliable he was … he should have stayed with her! Then, when she felt better, they could have searched together.

Jake frantically dashed toward her—avoiding rocks, stepping over roots, and swiping branches out of his way, dragging Katie until he heard Miranda's voice once more.

"Jake, I've found something." Her voice grew louder, and he slowed his pace, but Katie tugged him to a fast walk.

Relief coursed through him as he realized Miranda wasn't hurt or scared. Now that he knew she was safe, he was infuriated. She had to have known how dangerous it was to be wandering out here alone. Or maybe she didn't know. He had been teasing her about the dangers at night, after all, trying to ease her mind in the truck. He would regale her with all the dangers of being in the wilderness on her own when he caught up to her.

Miranda was guided by her nose. There was a slight breeze, and she drew in an odor similar to the one she'd smelled by Valerie on Saturday night. Taking Doc's leash, she carefully lifted her nose to the breeze, just like the times she'd seen her dog stretch his nose. Then she started moving in the direction of the scent. Because it was floating on the wind, she needed to pick one point and move toward it.

She'd been crouched down examining flowers when Jake burst through the brush, dragging Katie behind.

"Miranda, don't you know how dangerous it is to be out here on your own? Not only are there coyotes, mountain lions, bobcats, and bears but there are also smaller wildlife like skunks and porcupines. What if you got lost or injured?"

Miranda gently tugged him down to her level after he finished his tirade. The dogs stood still, neither even wagging a tail.

"Jake, nothing happened, and I have Doc with me. He would have at least barked if there had been some danger. But thank you for telling me what it's really like out here. I won't be so foolish again to go off on my own. Now, look at this." She pointed out plants that had been torn apart and strewn over the edge of a short cliff. "I let my nose bring me here. It's the same smell as was around Valerie. Do you remember it now?"

"I can't smell anything. Maybe if I go down closer. It's only about six feet, and it looks like there are some footholds along the way." Jake shrugged off his pack and climbed down. He took in a couple of deep breaths. "The scent is still very faint. How did you pick it up?"

"Maybe I'm more sensitive to it than you. But do you remember it now?" How could he not smell anything? It was so strong in her nostrils she thought she might gag.

"No, but I know what a couple of the flowers are. There are primroses, and this petal looks like an orchid. You may have found the flowers that had been planted in that covered soil patch we saw." Jake got a foothold and heaved himself back up onto the ledge. "I think we should go back and tell Nick."

"Why? You didn't really smell anything. The odors I have in my nose may just be a memory," she reasoned. But she was sure that somehow Valerie had been on these flowers, with them crushing against her, releasing their scent. How else would Valerie have carried this peculiar odor?

"I'm concerned about your reaction a little while ago. You almost fainted and had to sit for a while." He put out a hand to help her up.

She stood with Jake's help. "I was probably just overtired from the hike. It was steep, and I was winded but didn't want to say anything." Miranda didn't want to make more of her reaction than it deserved, but she sensed something was wrong. Very wrong.

"Miranda, you don't need to push yourself for me, but those reactions seemed a lot more than just being tired. I'm willing to stop and let you rest. Promise me you won't overdo again." Jake held both her shoulders, looking into her face. She was glad the cover of darkness hid the blush rising to her cheeks.

"Thanks, Jake. I appreciate that. Now, I think it's time to go home." Jake led with Katie, and Miranda and Doc followed. The hike back was filled with hooting owls, baying coyotes, and the breeze caressing the leaves. The moon's light still shone, accentuating the skeleton-like trees, those having lost most of their leaves.

They reached the truck without incident. Two tired dogs laid down on the back seat, closing their eyes almost immediately. The humans climbed in, too and then they left the area. It was still pretty early in the evening.

"How about stopping for dinner?" Jake asked. "I know a good Mexican restaurant. It's early, and I think we need to talk."

Miranda wanted to refuse and go home to hibernate against the questions he'd probably ask. There were things about the girls' disappearance and the threats from Val's stepfather that no one knew, and she wasn't about to say anything—yet. She might give in and tell Nick they'd found some torn flowers. The incident at the grocery store could be significant … maybe. She wanted to spend time with him, though, and that won out. And what did Jake think they needed to talk about? "I am hungry. That sounds good."

"Great, we'll be there in about 20 minutes."

"I'll relax and close my eyes if that's okay with you." She didn't want to start a conversation now; she needed to empty her mind of worries.

"I'll wake you when we get there."

A few minutes later, Miranda gently woke as she felt the slowing of the truck and heard the quiet rumble of the dogs still sleeping. She straightened in her seat. She couldn't believe she was going into a restaurant dressed so casually after a hike. She heard the quiet click of the blinker as they turned into the parking lot.

Jake turned off the ignition and left the cab to swing around and let Miranda out. He walked beside her, his hand warm and reassuring on her back, and as they approached the door, he reached out to open it. It somehow reminded her of Derek, the man she had thought she was going to marry. But Derek's gestures were always more possessive and for show she now realized. She was no judge of men and didn't want to fall into the same trap again, but Jake seemed so different.

They entered the restaurant, greeted by the spicy smell of salsa and sizzling fajitas. The host seated them at a booth where chips and salsa waited.

"Would you like anything to drink?" their quickly-appearing waiter asked.

"I'd like iced tea," Jake replied.

"I'd like hot tea," Miranda said. "I'm still a bit chilled, and something warm sounds good." The waiter nodded and left to get their drinks. Miranda picked up her menu.

"I think I'm going to have the steak fajitas. What are you having?" Jake set his menu near the edge for the waiter to pick up.

"Maybe a chicken taco," Miranda replied.

Their waiter appeared with the drinks and took out his pad. "Are you ready to order?"

"I am. I'll have the steak fajitas."

"I'll have the chicken taco salad with guacamole and no sour cream," Miranda said. When the waiter left, she faced Jake and asked, "What do we need to talk about?"

"Well ..." he looked sheepish. "I thought we could have our own debriefing session since you didn't seem to want to come to the official one."

"I suppose we could." Miranda drew out the words slowly. She was relieved the focus was removed from that night's events, or at least, she hoped it would be.

"We mostly talked about what went on inside us while we were processing the crisis at hand. So how did you feel? I noticed you had quite a reaction on Saturday... and almost the same reaction tonight."

"You're right there. Aren't you the observant one?" She needed to be more serious. "I'm sorry Jake," she continued. "Being flippant sometimes helps me relieve stress. It was quite a shock seeing someone I actually know almost dead. It brought back some of the memories of the girls when they were younger." Miranda unraveled the silverware from the napkin. "As for tonight's reaction, I can't understand. It makes no sense to me."

"The whole situation is distressing for me, too. It's the first time we've seen injuries this severe. I was able to talk it through with the group. Were you able to talk about it with your parents?" Jake folded his arms across his chest.

"No," she confessed. She wasn't going to talk about it with them, either. "I thought the authorities needed to find Valerie's parents first before my parents find out about it." She pulled the tea bag out of her cup and took a sip. It burned on the way down—punishment for her sins of omission?

"It seems strange that you hadn't seen Valerie around town. It's a pretty small community." Jake took a drink of his iced tea.

The waiter arrived, carrying their dinners to the table and interrupting them. Jake's fajitas sizzled and Miranda's taco salad emitted a zesty aroma. She bowed her head briefly and then picked up her fork. She took a bite of the chicken and salad dipped in guacamole.

"Do you always pray before eating?" Jake had stabbed a piece of steak and held his fork midway to his mouth while he asked the question.

"I forget sometimes, but mostly I try to remember. Even if it's a brief, 'thank you.'" She broke off some of the shell and dipped it in the salsa, glad the subject had changed from Valerie.

"My mom always insisted we pray before meals." Jake's eyes held regret, sadness, and then anger.

Miranda couldn't believe all the emotions in his eyes. She better be careful. What had happened to him?

"Why don't you see your mother very often?" She took another bite. Could it be because of her insisting on praying? Miranda hoped not.

"When I visit she thinks it's her duty to encourage me to go back to my old job, and then we have to go to church. I had a bad experience there as a kid, and I still find many churchgoers to be hypocrites and gossips. I don't want to be associated with them."

"I'm sorry. I had no idea. People can be cruel, even people who go to church." Miranda felt like a heel. Here she was praying, but at the same time holding back information which felt like a lie of omission. But she had good reasons for that. Suddenly, the meal wasn't so appetizing. She managed to take a few more bites for show.

"No, I'm the one that should be sorry," Jake said. "I didn't mean to give you the lowdown. Now—back to debriefing."

"Well, I don't have much more to say. But I do think you're right about telling Nick about the torn flowers we found and the overturned patch tonight. Will you be doing anymore scouting this week?" She was desperate to go out again in case Jenny, or a clue about her, was out there somewhere. She knew other capable teams would be out there, but she wanted to do something not sit and wait, and she did not want to go alone. There were pieces of a puzzle forming in her mind, but not enough to put them together yet.

"Yes, Nick has the whole week scheduled. We're on the schedule again tomorrow night, if you're game." He gave her a sheepish grin, maybe because he hadn't told her how often he'd had them scheduled. "Maybe this time, we can let the dogs off leash for a while."

"Doc could sure use the extra exercise, and he stays close when off leash most of the time." Miranda laid her napkin on the table and after ascertaining Jake was finished, too, stood to leave.

After paying, they left the restaurant, Jake's hand resting on the small of her back. That warm, cherished feeling zipped up her spine though she held herself as aloof from it as she could.

They clambered into the truck, and it wasn't long before Jake pulled into her driveway. He extracted Doc from the truck and Miranda leaped down. They walked to the door, and Miranda tugged the keys out of her pocket and unlocked the door. Jake hugged her and left.

As she walked in the house, a strange prickle moved up her spine. Was she being watched? Or was something about to happen?

CHAPTER NINE

TUESDAY, OCTOBER 22ND

MORNING

Miranda could almost smell the clean, crisp, and cold air she imagined would be surrounding the snow-draped mountaintops touched by the bright sunshine she viewed in the distance as she headed toward the office. This lovely picture was her commute each day as she traveled to work; whether the mountains were covered in clouds or bathed in sunshine, she could praise God for his majestic creation.

In spite of the inspiring view, she felt sluggish after a fitful night sleep. Her dreams had been plagued with visions of Valerie's still body, blood covering her lower back and her long blond hair fanned over her face, resting in the middle of a garden of torn flowers. In her dream, Miranda hid behind an old stump with a huckleberry bush growing out of it; she watched a shadow rip out the plants and shred the flowers before tossing them. Miranda had not been able to move but started trembling …

A long, loud buzz sounded in the car, interrupting Miranda's trance-like memory. Where was the noise was coming from? The car radio was off. The noise wouldn't quit! A car's honk alarmed her, and she slammed on the brakes; her stomach reached her throat, and she stopped just in time to avoid hitting a pedestrian in the crosswalk. The noise continued … now she recognized it was coming from her purse.

Her cell phone! She jerked it out and peeked at the screen. An AMBER Alert indicated that a three-year-old boy had been taken in a white Honda Civic. The pedestrian was now on the sidewalk, so Miranda started driving again.

Lord, thanks for protecting the pedestrian and bring the little boy safely home. Comfort his parents and give them the strength needed to endure through the time it takes to get their son back.

Memories flooded her, bringing her to the time when Jenny was three years old. Jenny was carefree and generous even at that young age. Miranda had been eleven years old then and hadn't minded at all when Jenny shadowed her. Miranda had been patient with the toddler, helping out their mother.

So the extreme change in behavior when Jenny turned fifteen had flummoxed Miranda. All of a sudden, Miranda had borne the brunt of Jenny's anger. Miranda had mentioned the problem to her parents, but as they hadn't seen any of the animosity, they passed it off as a teen change and told Miranda it would soon pass. Miranda was relieved to return to the peace of college and stopped coming home, except for holidays. Jenny and Valerie had run away at the end of one Thanksgiving break.

Miranda slowed her car and was about to park in her usual spot, but was disappointed to see another car already parked there. She was running behind schedule; fortunately, she found a parking place half a block away.

Miranda rushed to the building, swinging open the door, and then took the steps two at a time before crashing into the office. Rachel, her receptionist, stared open-mouthed as Miranda whisked by her with only a quick nod. She tugged off her coat and hung it on the coat tree in the corner near her desk. She sat down and opened the file on top of the stack on her desk. Her first appointment was a young married mother who wanted help with her marriage.

Lord, I'm late and in need of your wisdom to guide Stacy with her situation. Please give me your words of encouragement and direction. And Lord, please be with Jenny, keep her well and please prompt her to return to our family.

Miranda hadn't always prayed for Jenny, but with the returning memories prompted by the incidents of the last couple of days, Jenny was now forefront in Miranda's mind. Miranda took a moment to look around her office, focusing on the philodendron vines dangling from her desk, and the peace lily centered on the table between the armchairs against the opposite wall.

A picture of the lily petals, torn, danced in her mind, and the sense of evil once more sent a prickling sensation up her spine. Who had harmed Valerie? The man she'd seen at the grocery store or… Miranda bolted out of her chair, shoving it against the wall, and then paced, not wanting to let her mind go to—Jake. It couldn't have been him; he'd been with her the whole time. But … the flowers. She could detect the odor but he couldn't, or so he'd said. No, Jake had had nothing to do with the night-blooming flowers. It was merely her overactive mind. But… he did have a secret; of that, she was certain. It was her job to read people, after all.

A tentative knock at the door jolted her back to the present.

"Come in," Miranda said encouraging as she moved to open the door.

"Are you okay?" The young woman asked as she stepped into the room. She anxiously swept the room with her gaze.

"I'm alright." Miranda groaned inwardly, realizing her client probably heard and been startled by the bang of the chair. "I got up too quickly and pushed the chair into the wall. Have a seat." Miranda smiled and gestured to the chairs, trying to calm her nerves and prepare herself to listen to her client.

Miranda observed as Stacy fidgeting with her purse, her eyes darting around the office but not landing on anything.

"Stacy, what brings you here?" Miranda asked in a soothing tone. She wanted to ease Stacy's tension.

"I'm having problems in my marriage, and I want to know how to help it. I've written some things down." Stacy slipped a sheet of paper out of her purse and stretched her arm toward Miranda, holding the page out to her.

"Please, read it to me." Miranda leaned back, wanting to observe Stacy and also needing a little time to regain her composure.

"But ... but I ..." Stacy hesitated. "You really want me to read it?" Her gaze focused on the paper shaking in her hand.

"Yes." Miranda smiled as Stacy finally glanced up.

"Brad, he's my husband, likes his toys better than the kids and me." Stacy started slowly and then sped her way through the rest. "If I ask for anything like clothes for the children because they grow out of them so fast, he starts yelling and won't listen. I try to explain it's because they grew out of their clothes but he rants and swears, calling me horrible names, even if the girls are in the room! I noticed they run away when that happens, but I don't know where they go." Her eyes darted between the paper and Miranda.

"Your two girls run away when your husband yells?" She restated the question. "When do they come back?" Miranda willed her features not to express her deep concern over the situation. Anything could happen to those little girls and, after her sister had left, Miranda grew sensitive to children leaving anywhere without their parent's supervision or permission.

Miranda had heard these stories before; they were never easy to listen to, especially the ones about children so scared they ran until they couldn't hear the yelling anymore. Miranda had had adult clients who'd been a child in that situation, and there were long-term effects. They inevitably tried to win the love of the abusive parent and many times, especially girls would become involved with someone similar to that parent.

She still couldn't fathom why Jenny had left home. Neither of her parents was abusive, and they loved one another and had demonstrated that to their children too. *Why, Jenny?*

Her client answered her. "They come back after Brad has slammed out of the house and they hear his truck squeal down the road," Stacy hesitated a moment then asked. "Do you want me to get back to what I wrote?"

Miranda nodded, determined not to interrupt again until Stacy had finished. Stacy was beginning to lower her guard and show a little emotion. It was a good sign.

"Sometimes he leaves immediately but sometimes, well, he thinks I need to learn a lesson, and he shoves me around and hits or kicks me, leaving hidden bruises. I know he goes to another woman when he leaves." Stacy whispered that last part so softly Miranda almost missed her last words.

"How do you know that?" Miranda asked gently, her pen poised above her notepad.

"A friend from college saw him in the city, with a woman, and told me. But he just calls me to threaten divorce and then brags about the women he's been with, too, and then tells me how lacking I am." Stacy lifted her head and locked eyes with Miranda.

There was more and Miranda nodded to prompt Stacy to continue.

"I'm so scared when he leaves, hoping he'll come back and not leave for good. My girls wouldn't have a father then. But when he does return, we all walk on eggshells to keep the peace. I really think it's best that my kids have both a mother and father."

"A complete family is important to you. Did you grow up with both a mom and dad?" Miranda asked.

"Yes, and yes," Stacy said emphatically. She went on about the present and ignored the reference to her family. "Each time he comes back things are a little better, and I think maybe he'll stay. The girls and I keep our hands off his toys and the girls try to behave, hoping he will pay attention to them. But all he does is play computer games, watch

TV, or fly his remote planes. The girls cheering too noisily at the sight of the plane he was flying caused the last fight we had. He turned on me, with his eyes bulging and veins popping out. He threatened to burn down the house." She stopped abruptly. Bright color crept up her face. Her eyes still darted in all directions.

"Do you think he will follow through on his threat? Are you and the girls in danger?" Miranda broke the silence.

"No! He would never do anything to harm his family." Stacy's hot response in his defense reverberated around the room. "He must love us because he keeps coming back."

Miranda had to be careful. This woman was choosing to ignore the physical harm he caused her and the emotional harm to both the girls and herself. Most women don't worry about harm to themselves, but will protect their children.

"Would your husband be willing to attend counseling?"

"No, he did try once, but in words I won't repeat he said he wouldn't go again. Brad says I'm the one who needs the counseling, he's just fine and wouldn't get angry if it wasn't for my behavior."

Near the end of the appointment, Miranda wanted to introduce a way to keep her client and children safe if possible.

"Does your husband give any signs that his anger will escalate? Or do you get a sense that he is in the mood for a fight before it happens? I'm concerned for you and your girls' safety." Miranda let the silence linger as Stacy thought.

"Well … not that I can figure out. Sometimes an incident will go without a response and then the same thing will set him off at another time. It seems to come out of nowhere. I haven't paid much attention to my instincts." Stacy studied her hands.

"What do you think would happen if you told him the next time he starts yelling, that you and the girls were going out for a couple of hours until he calmed down?" Miranda lifted her eyes from the notepad.

"I don't have anywhere to go. I can't tell anyone I know what's going on at home. Isn't there some other way?" she asked, desperate.

"You already know what happens when you stay. The girls run out of the house, and we want to keep them safe. Would it be better for them to continue to hear the fights or to go to the mall for a few hours with you and look around? Hopefully, when you return home, your husband will have calmed," Miranda explained.

"I suppose we could go to the mall or the park. Maybe the girls could play with the other kids there." Stacy's expression seemed both hopeful and unsure.

"I have one other suggestion. It might help to keep a journal expressing your feelings during the next week. You may see a pattern, or start to realize you really can sense if another fight is imminent."

"I've never had a journal," Stacy responded.

"You can use any notebook. Don't worry about what you write, just jot down what comes to mind. Have you made an appointment for next week yet?" Miranda moved to the edge of her seat, ready to get up.

"I did make an appointment. But I don't have money to continue for long. Brad has control of all the money." Her face reddened as she stood.

"Don't worry about the money. We'll discuss that later. I'm looking forward to seeing you next week." Miranda stood and followed Stacy to the door. She opened it and gave Stacy a reassuring smile as she left.

Lord, give this young woman the strength she needs to move forward through the difficult path ahead. Keep the girls safe, too, Lord. Give me wisdom at each session. Amen.

Miranda reflected on her own family. Her parents loved and were involved in all their kids' lives, yet Jenny left and was still gone. Stacy's husband was abusive, and the little girls left but came back when it was calm in the house again. Families were so complicated.

The rest of the day went pretty smoothly. On her way out, she noticed Rachel had set up the Christmas cactus on a table under the window next to the water cooler.

"The plant looks nice there near the window," Miranda commented.

"I agree, it needs some sunlight and gives the office a lived-in feel. We could use a few more plants in here. Would you like me to pick up a couple? My girls love choosing flowers so it wouldn't be a problem." Rachel shut down her computer, preparing to leave with Miranda.

"Yes, do that and bring in the receipt. I'll reimburse you tomorrow or when you have a chance to go. But remember, I have plants in my office that don't need care for a reason." Miranda warned with a smile.

"Oh, that's okay I love tending plants. Have a nice evening." Rachel left ahead of Miranda.

On her way home, Miranda thought about the night ahead, anticipating the hike with trepidation. She was certain there would be nothing nice about the coming evening. She still had a gut feeling something bad was going to happen.

CHAPTER TEN

TUESDAY, OCTOBER 22ND

EVENING

Miranda plunged the key into the lock, expecting to hear whining and scratching on Doc's crate as she stepped inside. But to her dismay, Miranda heard nothing.

With his parents' permission, she had engaged a boy to let the dog out a couple of times during the day. That particular family homeschooled their kids, and they allowed for some flexibility with their son's school day so he could let the dog out. Today, she'd left Doc at home and had hired the young man to come over. Had he lost her dog somehow?

Miranda quickly went up the stairs, hoping nothing was wrong. She stared at an empty crate and then called his name in a panic. "Doc, Doc, come!" She hadn't expected an answer, but she yelled anyway.

Miranda bolted downstairs, through the hallway, and into the kitchen. She swung open the back door and was struck by the cold air on her face and paws into her stomach. "Ohhh!" She said, breathing out and losing her balance. She fell back but hung onto the door jamb, which allowed her to remain standing. As she bent over to catch her breath, her dog licked her face. Someone stood behind Doc.

"Doc—off!" Russell, the dog's ten-year-old pet sitter commanded in his most serious voice. "I'm so sorry Miss Jacobsen. I was late for the last visit, and so I played a little longer than normal. Are you okay?"

She coughed and managed a smile and a nod.

"Thanks, Russell, I'm fine, just surprised by the enthusiastic 'hello' from Doc. How are you doing today? The two of you were so quiet I thought something was wrong."

"Well, other than being late I'm doing good. I'd better get home, or I'll be late for dinner, too. Bye." Russell dashed through the gate and back to his house.

"Come here, monster," Miranda said in a voice reserved for pets and babies. "We need to eat and get ready for another hike tonight. Katie will be coming soon." At the word Katie, Doc's high-pitched shepherd growl-talk started and didn't stop until Miranda managed to put down a dish of food for him.

She picked at an already-prepared chicken Caesar salad but wasn't very hungry. She couldn't shake the feeling that something was wrong. Maybe she was nervous about going out again with Jake. No. it wasn't Jake. She couldn't put her finger on it.

She'd had this feeling once a long time ago. She had sensed something wrong while accompanying her family home from the movies. That feeling of foreboding was so strong that Miranda hadn't wanted to go into the house, but her father had insisted she get out of the car.

They had entered the house frozen in shock—not a sound was heard from any of them. Drawers had been emptied, cushions were thrown around the room, pictures and knick knacks had been pulled off the walls and books were strewn on the floor. They had been robbed.

Doc's barking jolted Miranda to the present and alerted her to Jake and Katie's arrival. Miranda slipped the salad back in the refrigerator then went to open the door.

"Hi." Jake's warm smile, his white teeth contrasting with his dark beard, greeted her. She lifted her eyes and melted into his calm, coffee-eyed gaze.

She stepped back to prevent herself from naturally leaning toward him. She couldn't let her guard down yet.

"Come on in, Jake. We were just finishing up dinner and gathering essentials for the pack." Miranda stepped aside, allowing Jake room to enter. They walked to the kitchen while the dogs trotted, with Doc pushing Katie in the face to get her to play. The dogs were so carefree; Miranda envied them. Humans were so … complicated. Her life was full of distrust and bottled-up fears that kept her quiet until she felt she was at the bursting point. *Lord, is Jake my sounding board?*

"I called Nick today and told him about the flowers we found. He said he would check it out today. And he said so far the park is clear of any other signs, but he wants us to be cautious. He doesn't think the perpetrator is still out there, but he doesn't want anyone going out alone."

"Are you sure we should go?" Miranda was having second thoughts, even though she wanted to make sure her sister wasn't out there.

"Hey, we have the dogs with us, too. We're a small group; I think we'll be fine." Jake gently grasped her arm and turned her toward him. He took her other arm and fixed his gaze on hers. Then, to her surprise, he brought her close and embraced her. She thought she heard him whisper, "I'll protect you."

Maybe I can trust him. What about it God? You can drop a "yes" out of the sky.

Miranda wanted to believe him and held on tight, letting his steady breathing quiet her erratic heart. The dogs quickly interrupted this short interlude.

"I'm ready." Miranda grabbed her pack and Doc's leash and then they left. Once settled, she asked Jake how his day had gone. She wasn't ready to talk.

Jake entertained her with his recount of the day's work. This time of the year was slow for landscaping, so he needed to generate some more work. He'd gone to different floral shops, giving out his business card and trying to solicit work with businesses that needed care for the flora in their buildings.

"I asked about the flowers we found at some of the florists. There are only two places here that sell night-blooming flowers, and neither has sold any since the beginning of the summer." Jake glanced at Miranda and then back at the road again. "I thought someone might have bought them here in town, but I think I'm wrong. Come to think of it, I don't service anyone with night-blooming flowers."

"Would you have to work at night if you did?" Miranda held in her laughter until he looked at her, and then she erupted. Jake joined in, followed by the dogs' howling. Tension had been released, and a peace occupied its place.

"Okay, enough already. Now it's your turn to tell me about your day." Jake seemed to try for a solemn tone, but couldn't quite pull it off.

"You realize the joke pointed more toward my ignorance and lack of plant knowledge, and not toward making fun of the work you do."

"I know, and truly I have a sense of humor and can be teased. Really, how did your day go?"

"I started the day with a new client. I, too, need a few new clients before I have a full schedule. I work every day, but sometimes have afternoons completely off. As a matter of fact, I have tomorrow afternoon off. I need about six to twelve new clients to be completely booked. I'm doing okay and can afford to have a receptionist, but eventually, I'd like to bring in another therapist. That way, the office wouldn't have to shut down for vacations, and I could increase Rachel's salary. She does a great job, and I'm well aware that she has three cute little girls to support." The peace hadn't lifted. Miranda continued to talk, and as she did, she stared at Jake's profile. From time to time he'd glance at her with his crooked smile. *Is this your answer of yes, God? Or is it wait?*

The dogs' whining preceded their entering the parking lot. The truck stopped, and everyone unloaded. With packs on they were ready to start.

"We're going up a different trail tonight, and at the end of it is a spectacular view of the stars," Jake said. "It's wide open. We'll keep the dogs' leashes on going up and if we don't spot anyone we can let them run free a little on the way down. Let's go." The trail was wide enough to allow them to walk side by side.

The moon wasn't as bright tonight; it had been shaved down over the past three nights—almost four—but the sky was clear of any clouds. With flashlight beams illuminating their path, they forged ahead.

Doc's ears pricked but he behaved on leash. He'd pounce off to the side once in a while but always came up empty.

"What do you suppose Doc is trying to trap? I don't see Katie attacking the brush off to the side like Doc is," Miranda pointed out.

"I'm not sure what he sees. Maybe it's just a leaf flicking, and he thinks something is there. I've started teaching Katie to ignore wildlife so she can turn into a wilderness search dog. To do that, she needs to concentrate on human scent and leave all others alone. That may be why she isn't behaving the same way. But they are two different dogs, and won't behave in the same way." Jake twined his fingers with Miranda's.

"Like humans." She rolled her eyes. "All different. I wonder what wildlife should I be afraid of at night?" The grade grew steeper, and they started on the switchbacks. Miranda became a little breathless.

"There are lions and tigers and bears." Jake's tone teased. "Well, there aren't any tigers. But there are mountain lions, some bears, coyotes, and skunks and a few other animals like raccoons, opossums, and porcupines. You want to be careful around all of them, but with our lights flashing and the noise we make talking it should be pretty safe. Besides, I'm here to defend you," Jake said with bravado, but then he stopped her, and they listened.

Besides the owls hooting and the whisper of the wind, she heard something moving swiftly through the woods, kicking up the fallen leaves. A musky, pungent scent hung on the breeze as they watched a six-point buck soar by effortlessly.

Miranda gasped at the awesome display of God's creation in action. What a stunning animal! "Wow," was the only word she could get out.

"They are amazing aren't they? Let's get going." Jake urged them forward.

Other than the night whispers and the hooting owls, they only heard, but didn't see, one other animal moving through the brush.

At the end of the trail, the expanse of the heavens opened up as Jake had promised. Millions of twinkling stars shone. Miranda tried looking for the familiar constellations she had learned from her father when she'd been a small girl. It had been easy when they were the brightest without the backdrop of all the sparkling lights in the sky, but with the mass of stars out tonight, she had a hard time identifying any specific constellations.

She sat on a flat rock and Jake dropped next to her and then leaned in, pressing against her side. Warmth seeped through her as she leaned against his strong arm.

"It's spectacular isn't it?" His warm breath caressed her ear.

"It is," she exhaled the two words without moving her gaze. "Look! A shooting star." *Lord, what a glorious creation. I think this was your yes for me. Give me the right words. Amen.* "Does something like this make you think about God?" she dared ask.

"It makes me realize there is a God. But I'm not about to trust him. Too many Christians have disappointed me. I see gossips and hypocrites in the church too often. If you can't trust a Christian, who can you trust? So, I haven't been on speaking terms with God for a long time."

"Wow, but you're right. People often disappoint us, and I'm sure I've disappointed friends and family too." Guilt clogged her brain, and she wasn't able to think beyond her shortcomings. Who was she to talk about Christ? She had secrets and fears of letting the truth be known. *And the truth will set you free.* Right. But how many lives could be hurt if she divulged her secrets? Admittedly, probably only her own pride. "Christ can't fail us. He never changes," she said as much to herself as to Jake.

"Maybe not, but his followers can be cruel," Jake stated in a matter-of-fact tone.

"You're right about that. The night Jenny and Valerie ran away, I was that cruel person. Jenny and I both said vicious things to one another. I've held in the guilt for so long its part of me. I guess even

I'm not the person you thought I was, am I? My parents don't even know how terrible we were to one another. I blame myself for Jenny's leaving. When my parents look at me, I feel ashamed, and that's one reason I've kept my distance, although we still talk and I often go for dinner. I know God forgives me, but I need to find Jenny and ask her forgiveness." Silence followed her confession. Had she heard God right and had been supposed to speak up? Or had she just pushed Jake away?

An arm slowly engulfed her shoulders and Jake drew her close. Her throat clogged and tears dripped down her cheeks. She hadn't known Jake for very long, but her attraction to this outdoorsman was stronger than it had ever been with Derek, the ex-fiancé in Seattle.

"Miranda, it took courage to say what you just confessed. I don't think less of you." He laid his cheek on the top of her head.

Miranda swiped away the tears with her sleeve and sat up.

"Thank you," she choked out. "I think we should get back." A weight had been lifted from her shoulders. Still, she wondered what had caused his hurt and what kind of cruelty had he endured and still held inside.

"We can let the dogs off-leash here," Jake said as he released the clip from Katie's collar.

Miranda did the same with Doc, and both dogs shot off. Less than a minute later they came bounding back for a pat and a "good dog" from them both. Miranda gave each dog a treat to ensure Doc's return next time, especially, and the dogs took off once more.

Jake curled his hand around Miranda's. "The dogs are having a great time." They could hear the barking dogs in the distance. Jake whistled, and both came sprinting back. Again, both got a treat.

They took off once more, but a few minutes later, the tone of their barking changed. Katie returned, rushing up to Jake and bouncing off him before charging off again. Doc followed Katie, but the next time the little black Katie dog came back there was no Doc following her.

"Doc!" Miranda yelled in alarm. "Where is he? We need to find him." Miranda began running ahead almost blindly.

"Miranda, wait." Jake caught up to her. "Maybe Katie will get us to him. Search, Katie." Jake gave her the command. Katie took off. "Listen." Jake held Miranda still.

"I hear growling. Do you think he's up against some wildlife? He's just a pup, Jake." She tugged away and started running in the direction of the noise.

Jake again caught up to the distraught Miranda. "Miranda let me lead. You don't even know what he may be up against. I've had some experience. Trust me."

"You're right, but hurry. Please," she pled. There wasn't an option but to trust Jake.

Katie ran back and bounced off Jake again. Jake grabbed Miranda's hand, and they followed his dog. They slowed down in the heavy brush and finally, breathless, they stopped.

Miranda bent over, trying to catch her breath, but soon lifted her eyes to see Doc crouched and growling. She couldn't see what he was growling at, but he didn't seem to be in any danger. She released a sigh and gradually rose to a stand. Then the tingling started up her back and down her arms again.

Something was wrong. She felt light-headed and had to sit.

"What is it Jake?" she asked, her voice wavering. Doc must have sensed her need as he trotted to lean against her. Miranda clung to the dog.

Jake hadn't answered. Something must be wrong. Using her dog for balance, Miranda stood on shaky legs. Jake bent over, looking intently at something. He must not have heard her approach because he jumped when she touched his shoulder.

"Miranda we need to back out of here and stay away. I need to call Nick." Jake jumped up and grasped Miranda's elbow to turn her around. He did—but not before she saw a pair of tennis shoes.

CHAPTER ELEVEN

TUESDAY, OCTOBER 22ND

NIGHTTIME

"**M**iranda we can't go near the body. The police need to inspect the area, and they'll need a medical examiner to examine the body. We need to stay clear." Jake wasn't having an easy time holding back the determined woman.

"But that could be my sister," Miranda wailed. "I need to see who it is." She strained against his strong hold, but he had to keep her away.

"Miranda, let me call 911. The sooner we get the police here, the sooner you'll know if it's your sister. No matter what, we need to leave the scene untouched." He hoped to break through her stubborn resolve to see if the body was indeed her sister, a body covered with brambles with only the feet in tennis shoes sticking out to be seen.

He needed to guard the crime scene and already had the dogs on their leashes that he'd then tied to a couple of young trees not far from them.

Miranda finally stopped struggling and in a defeated tone announced, "You're right. I'll sit here."

Jake could tell she was only remaining there under duress. He couldn't blame her for wanting to know who was lying there, especially after her confession earlier. If he had seen repentance like Miranda had expressed tonight any time in his early church days, he might have believed God truly cared for him. That hadn't been his experience.

He'd prayed the fighting between his parents would stop, and it did—the night his father left. His father had then married one of his associates the day after the divorce was final. God hadn't seen fit to keep his family together in spite of his prayers.

Jake and his mom continued to attend the same church for a while, but the gossip and rumors had run rampant. The gossips had blamed Jake's mom for the break-up and predicted Jake would follow in his father's footsteps. Jake had prayed for those Christians to open their eyes and see the truth of the situation, to be compassionate and forgiving as the Bible instructs. Instead, they all but shunned mother and son, forcing them to leave the church. Jake hadn't gone back to any church since then.

He'd purposefully become the opposite of his father. Jake had enjoyed hiking with his mother and decided to live a casual lifestyle. His father was a businessman, dressed in a suit and tie, working for a corporation. Jake owned a sole-proprietor business and dressed down to work in the dirt. His father had styled hair and was clean-shaven while Jake let the hair on his head and his face grow. Regretfully, his mother couldn't understand why Jake had left the city and a potentially well-paying job. Jake had kept the animosity he felt toward his father to himself.

The heavy footfalls coming up the trail brought him back to the present. Pete Sweete bustled into view first, followed by three other officers. Jake noticed that Pete saw him sitting next to Miranda, his arm around her shoulders, as they perched on an old log about thirty feet from the scene. Doc and Katie were lying down watching the activity.

"Jake and Miranda again," Deputy Sweete loudly accused. Sweete reminded Jake of a bulldog; his stocky frame lumbered toward them. His brows knit together in a straight line across his forehead. The brows were level with the bill of the cap that hid Sweete's shaven head. Jake pointed in the direction of the victim, and the other three officers went to work. But Pete stayed right where he'd planted his feet.

One of the other officers started putting up the crime scene tape and the other crime scene techs started processing the area.

"The last time we were called to the scene because I'm an EMT. So this is technically the first time we two actually found something." Jake didn't like what Pete's tone implied. The deputy had ticketed Jake for going three miles over the speed limit on an empty rural road not long after Jake moved to Stone Ridge. From that time forward they'd been civil to one another, but not friendly.

Pete's path seemed to cross Jake's path, at least two to three times a week. Jake was sure it was on purpose. The deputy always had some derogatory remark about Jake's long hair or his beard.

"Can you go see who is lying there?" Miranda's demand interrupted Jake's thoughts.

"Why? Do you know who it is?" Sweete's tone had a challenge to it.

"No. I hope not," Miranda hesitantly answered.

"Tell me what you two are doing here. First you were at the scene Saturday night. Then you found the flowers last night. Now you're here again. I knew something like this would happen some day with you, Jake. Miranda, you'd better be careful."

Jake's brows shot up. If he hadn't been holding Miranda, he might have … he'd better not think about doing something that would play into the man's hands. "How did you know about the flowers?"

"I was in the office when the call came in last evening. Detective Ryker was also working late," Sweete answered.

"I think we'll wait and talk with Nick. He can tell you what we are doing out here." Jake didn't move his gaze from Pete's. There were times the deputy rubbed him the wrong way, and this was one of them. Sweete had been in the office when the detective had scheduled the groups for park surveillance, so he should know why the two of them were out here, anyway.

"Detective Ryker won't be here for an hour and …"

"Miranda and I can wait," Jake interrupted.

"Suit yourself. I'm sure the detective will want answers, too."

Nick wouldn't believe that they'd had anything to do with the two victims. He definitely wouldn't—would he? Two victims … might a third turn up? Jake tightened his hold on Miranda.

"Jake, is something wrong?" She tried to wiggle free.

"Well, I'm worried." His stomach clenched at the thought of something happening to Miranda. His fingers dug into Miranda's arm. All he wanted to do was protect her—nothing more.

"Jake." She leaned close and whispered. "What's going on? Can you loosen your grip on my arm please?"

"Sorry. I just thought that there are already two victims and …" He stopped, not wanting to voice his fear that Miranda might be in danger, too. After all, she knew the first victim and maybe she knew this one, too. He'd been fighting his growing attraction and was losing the battle. He'd have to make sure nothing happened to Miranda and then steel himself from any other thoughts about her, or about them together. It couldn't work out; he'd already failed her. If it hadn't had been for him, they'd never have been out on Saturday night, Monday night, or even now. There couldn't be a God out there, not with all this tragedy and stress placed on Miranda. If there was a God, would he have let this happen?

In black clothes and a knit beanie, he blended with the shadows of the rocky ledge, high above the activity below. The body had been found before he'd had a chance to leave. The barking dogs had warned him that he needed to find a place to hide … and quickly. Fortunately, growing up with a father who hunted and who had taught him techniques to avoid detection from wildlife had been put to good use that night.

Lifting the binoculars, he stared at the pair on the log. The officer had almost bellowed their names in a condemning tone. All the better;

it would lead the police on a rabbit trail and thereby give him time to figure out his next step.

Hmm, Miranda. A familiar name from … it came to him in a flash. Yes! The business card he'd extracted from the clerk had belonged to Miranda Jacobsen. Were they one and the same?

He wasn't too worried about the police; they would soon figure out the place the body had been found wasn't the scene of the crime. They'd take the body and go. Instead, he focused in on the woman sitting on the log. He'd seen that face before … in the grocery store squatting behind a display of Christmas cactus, that's where he'd seen her! Was she the Miranda on the business card? Did it matter? This Miranda could identify his latest victim—and possibly him.

His father had taught him to protect his assets, and he had a side business that paid six figures. He wasn't going to let anything or anyone interfere with that. He'd already taken care of two of the problems and now, nearly a third. He could dispose of the third soon. He wouldn't have even had to go down this road if his stepbrother hadn't started listening to his girlfriend, Valerie. She had the boy convinced to get help for his drug addiction and then expose the dealer who had been selling him the drugs for years.

His stepbrother, Jared, had told him, hoping for a pat on the back. Instead, he'd given Jared a lethal dose. Jared hadn't known who was behind the drug dealer. Him. A patient man, he waited to find the right way and time to take care of Valerie. He wasn't sure exactly what she knew, but couldn't take any chances.

How was he to know Valerie had bragged to another clerk about her night excursion? So now he'd had to take care of that problem, too. He had been careful. He was sure he hadn't left anything to incriminate himself.

He was determined not to make any mistakes this time. He'd be patient and plan carefully. He looked down at the scene once more.

"Hey, where are you two going?" one of the officers yelled.

"I'm taking Miranda to the truck to get warm." Jake held both leashes in one hand and Miranda's arm in the other.

"But …"

"Don't worry, I'll wait for the detective and show him up here."

Hmm, maybe I won't have to plan too far in advance. It all depends on whether everyone else stays by the body long enough.

CHAPTER TWELVE

TUESDAY, OCTOBER 22ND

LATE NIGHT

"**M**iranda, are you sure you want to go back to the truck?" Jake held the dogs' leashes as they continued down the trail. They were not far from the parking lot.

She heard the crunch of gravel as more cars arrived; presumably, Detective Ryker and the medical examiner were earlier than expected. Headlights lit up the night and all the noise drowned out any sound wildlife might make.

"Jake, I'll be fine. The dogs will be in the truck with me, and I *will* leave the doors locked. I may run the engine for a short time to heat up the inside." She had been so adamant to see the victim, but now she was having second thoughts. A chill ran up her spine. She'd confessed she was cold, so they'd trekked down. But cold feet had caused her shivering, and now she could not bear the thought that it might be her sister lying there—dead. And, she'd had the ominous impression of someone watching her.

"It sounds pretty busy down there," Jake commented. "I wonder what's going on?"

Nick met them a few yards before Jake and Miranda had reached the lot. He had made it earlier than expected. "The media are here. Where are you two going?"

"Miranda is cold and needs to get warm. Thought she could wait in the truck for a while," Jake answered.

"Okay, but Miranda, I will need to talk with you as well and get your statement." Nick's tone was stern.

"Sure."

"As far as the media goes, either ignore the questions or say 'no comment.' Got it? Nothing gets out to the media."

Jake and Miranda nodded in unison.

"I'll be back up as soon as I get Miranda situated," Jake informed the detective as he and Miranda continued to the truck.

Miranda imagined there might be microphones headed their way until the reporters caught sight of the dogs, and then they'd probably back off but would still yell out questions. "Do you know the victim? A male or female? How did you find the victim? Were the dogs involved?"

However, there were only a couple reporters, and most likely from newspapers because she didn't see any vans with TV stations listed. One of the reporters asked if they knew anything about the victim, and when both Jake and Miranda shook their heads, the reporters continued to get ready to hike up the trail.

Finally, Miranda reached Jake's truck with Jake, and the dogs close behind.

"Why didn't the reporter push any harder? I thought they'd try harder to get information." She stood with her hand on the door handle and head tilted up to face Jake.

"I don't know. Maybe they thought we didn't know anything since we weren't at the scene. Nick already told them that nothing would be said. I think going up there is pretty pushy." Jake opened the back door and let the dogs jump inside.

"I'll be alright with the dogs and the doors locked," she reminded Jake as she hefted herself up. "Besides, the barking will scare anyone from coming if there *is* someone out there. Why would anyone want to have anything to do with me?" she asked. She wasn't about to confess to Jake her intuition. *Was it intuition? Or was it God's prodding, telling her someone was—maybe—stalking her?*

"Do you have your cell turned on?" Jake leaned in and gently touched his lips to hers.

"Uh-huh," was all she could muster. She forced out the next words. "I'm cold and tired, and my cell is on a loud ring. Go ahead, they need you out there." What she really wanted to say was, *Please stay.*

"Remember to turn off the truck before you fall asleep." He turned and started toward the trail.

"I will. Hurry back." Miranda leaned her head back, watching Jake's retreat. She touched her lips and closed her eyes. There had been so much emotion in his gentle touch.

Miranda had only intended to rest until she was warm, but suddenly her head jerked, and her eyes flew open. The warm cab smelled of dog breath, and when she lit up her watch she'd realized she'd been asleep for fifteen minutes. She turned off the engine and listened to the rhythmic snoring of the dogs.

Regret closed her throat. She shouldn't have left the scene. If the victim was Jenny, she had to know; if it wasn't her sister, who was it? *Lord, I pray that's not Jenny up there, but I'm having a hard time dealing with anyone being a victim. Please find the perpetrator before anyone else is attacked. Do you want me to go back?* Oh, how she wished he would answer quickly. Maybe a "yes" or "no" printed in the steam on the windows.

Well, God probably wasn't going to print on the windows, so what should she do in the meantime? How long would they be up there? It could be a long time, and Miranda wavered between needing to know who the victim was up there and wanting to remain safe. She pulled the keys out of the ignition and quietly opened the door, trying to leave the dogs undisturbed. She couldn't handle both dogs, and didn't think it fair only to bring one of them. Miranda made sure the truck was locked, and with resolve, she straightened her shoulders and lifted her head before proceeding to the trailhead.

The parking lot was quiet and dark. Several vehicles were outlined in the moon's glow, but as she moved under the trees, she realized she'd need her flashlight. Oh, she'd forgotten it in the truck. Should she go back? She froze when she heard the rustling in the brush off to her left. Could it be a deer, or maybe something more dangerous, like a bear? She'd better move. Her mind tried to make her feet move, but they wouldn't cooperate at first. Then she heard her name mumbled, along with other words. Her feet left the ground.

Miranda tried to slow her racing heart as she slowly and as quietly as possible moved to the right. Could it have been Jake who'd spoken her name? No, he'd take the trail. Anyone else would likely take the trail, too. So who had known her name, and why had he said it aloud?

The tingling started again, and panic wanted to take over. She needed to think and calm the panic. She took a deep breath. What had Jake taught her? She took another deep breath. She couldn't remember, but needed to hide now. *Oh Lord, please hide me, find a refuge for me. Keep the wildlife away and whoever had said my name, too.* She took another deep breath.

It was dark, and she had no flashlight. Unexpectedly, she fell over a fallen log! She held still. A hooting owl was all she heard. She felt around and decided this is where she'd stay for the moment. She'd fallen in the corner of two moss-covered fallen logs arranged in a V shape.

She held her breath and listened. Miranda jumped at the ferocious sound of the dogs barking. She should go back, but what if that person was there? Oh, she didn't know what to do. *Stay.* She had the distinct impression that she should stay. *God, I hope that was from you.*

He stopped, still hidden in the brush, but with a view of the parking lot. No one was in sight, so the professor slowly moved forward.

He flashed his beam into each of the empty cars but saw no one. He recognized the detective's car and the rest were marked as media, so that left the Dodge. *Fate must be on my side. All I have to do is lure her out, and my problems will be over. I've covered my tracks, and nothing could lead to me.*

He stealthily approached the truck. He didn't see her right away, but she could have been sleeping, so he slowly raised his head and directed the beam toward the seat. Gone. He shot back when the dogs pounced on the window barking viciously. Then, a slow smile formed as he realized they couldn't get to him. The girl couldn't have gone far. He'd have seen her if she'd returned on the trail. He had kept the trail in sight all the way down and not one person crossed his path. Could he lure her out from wherever she hid?

"Miranda, where are you? I have to talk to you about Valerie," he called. Ahhh … that should get her attention.

No answer. He silently progressed to the trailhead and was about to call again, but the tromping and muffled voices of several people came toward him.

He would finish the job, just not as soon as he had hoped. He was a patient man.

Miranda stayed motionless. She'd heard her name again—and Valerie's. Who was this guy, and what did he want with her? How did he know Valerie? The dampness of the ground seeped through her clothes, and she shivered from the cold. She was not dressed for a stakeout in the woods. *Jake, please come back.*

What if Jake did come back and the man whispering her name attacked him? No, she wouldn't consider such a thing. After this was over, hiking was something she was going to avoid for a while. Quite a while.

She listened and heard voices and boots scuffing in the dirt. Should she go meet the people in those boots, using those voices, falling in with

MURDER BLOOMS AT NIGHT

the others? Actually, she couldn't if she wanted to; her joints were stiff from the cool, damp, needle-and-moss bed. Some of the pine needles had worked their way through her pants. To avoid the pricking, she shifted position.

Well, do I move now? She heard, *Stay!* It seemed a directive, so she stayed. That wasn't easy, even though she was wide-awake now. She shifted from side to side to avoid the jabbing needles. Her aching joints complained, and her wet clothes clung to her, chilling her right through.

Miranda closed her eyes and focused on Jake and his gentle kiss, which kept her mind off her current situation. He would come for her.

A cold, wet nose pressed against her cheek, and she almost flipped over the log. She hadn't heard any barking or rustling in the brush, how could she have missed it? She ventured to open her eyes to see what creature had found her. She stared into the round amber eyes of her dog, felt the warm puffs on her face as he panted.

"Doc, how did you get here? Why didn't I hear you?" She often talked to her dog without expecting a reply.

"We weren't all that quiet," Jake answered, climbing over the log before sitting next to Miranda. "What are you doing out here? I didn't know my heart could jump up into my throat until I looked into an empty truck. Miranda, why are you here?" Jake stretched his legs in front of himself, then crossed them at the ankles.

"I decided I wanted to see if the victim was my sister, so I left the truck." Miranda drew her knees to her chest. "Did you ... see any strangers in the parking lot?" She couldn't keep what happened a secret.

"No, why?"

"Well the reason I'm here on the ground," she spoke slowly, "is because I was on my way to you when I heard someone speak my name and then said some other mumbling. Someone was on the other side of the trail. I needed to hide and went in the opposite direction." She hugged Doc, but the dog struggled to get free from her strangling embrace.

"Did you see anyone?" Jake's voice reflected concern.

"No, but the dogs were barking loud enough for me to hear them through the closed truck windows, and then the voice called my name. Oh Jake, I was so afraid, but I stayed here and didn't move because I had the impression God was telling me to stay. I think I'm frozen in this position." She rubbed her arms.

Jake, ever practical, didn't mention God but stood and held out his hand to help her up. "Let's get back to the truck. Maybe Nick will postpone your statement until tomorrow. Come on, let's go. I'll turn on the heat; you look cold."

"That man could still be out there Jake. We need to be careful and watch to see if we are followed." She cringed in pain as she straightened her rigid joints.

"We'll be okay. I think, I think this is a time you should pray."

He was right. She would pray, but she also couldn't help wonder where the man might show up next time. She had the uncanny feeling he'd turn up soon.

CHAPTER THIRTEEN

WEDNESDAY, OCTOBER 23RD

EARLY MORNING

Miranda shed the damp clothing, donned her fleece pajamas, and slipped under the heavy quilt to quell the chill: not only the physical chill but also the chill deep inside that a stranger knew her—and Valerie. Maybe she should have talked with that man, answered him, but the still, small voice had said *Stay*. But maybe … it was too late now. He might show up somewhere else and answer some of her questions.

The trip home had been quiet. Jake had seemed to sense her need for space. He was a thoughtful man, but he was an *outdoorsman,* and right now she didn't want to see another beautiful sight in the wilderness; she was done with wilderness. She had declined his dinner invitation for the coming evening. He'd graciously accepted her answer, and said he'd be in touch. She truly hoped he would call sometime, but right now, she needed some time to think, alone.

It was 1:00 a.m. She turned over one more time and closed her eyes. She had a half-day workload ahead of her, and then would be expected at the police station to give her statement. Her evening, however, would be free. She'd turned down Jake because if he asked her to go on a hike afterward, she was almost certain she would break down and accept, but she did not think she could face one more.

Her cell phone rang, and her eyes popped open. Caller ID showed "unknown." Should she answer it? She had given her personal cell number to a very select few of her clients. Maybe one of them needed a listening ear? After the fourth ring, she answered it only to hear a click. Maybe she hadn't been quick enough to answer, or maybe the client had decided it was, well, too early in the morning for a call. Miranda closed her eyes once more before finally falling into a dreamless sleep.

Ring, ring, ring. She woke once more. Maybe it was her client calling back. It was an unknown caller again, and Miranda swiped the phone to answer. "Hello, who is this?"

There was nothing but heavy breathing on the other end.

"Hello, is this someone I know?" she tried again.

"No, but I know *you*, Miranda," whispered a gruff, raspy voice. Then "click" and the phone went dead once more.

Who could that have been? She racked her brain. Which client might have a disgruntled husband or friend? It could have been Stacy's husband … or could it have been the man who'd called her name last night. A chill raced up and down her spine.

Miranda flung off her quilt and sprang out of bed, slid into her slippers, and unlatched Doc's crate. *No use in going back to sleep now.* Both dog and owner slogged to the kitchen. Miranda dragged out the coffee pot, filled it with water, and let it perk, then let Doc out.

She had a desperate urge to call Jake, but it was only 4:00 a.m. After she'd declined his invitation to dinner the night before, would he even be happy to hear from her so soon? She gradually calmed down and remembered she was going to give her statement that afternoon. Maybe she could talk with the detective then. After some time had passed with no more calls, she decided she could wait. Maybe the calls were connected to Valerie and Jenny.

The rich aroma of the dark brew filled the kitchen and Miranda breathed in deeply. She poured a cup and sipped the hot liquid. Cup in hand, she ambled to open the door for Doc. He was wide-awake and nudged Miranda before walking to his bowl.

"It doesn't matter what time of day it is, you're always hungry. Hang on." She stooped to pick up his bowl. The high-pitched sound of the clinking of the food dropping into the metal bowl helped ground her morning. Miranda continued through her normal routine. It was still early, so she took extra time to read her Bible, remembering what she knew to be true. God was in control, and he was with her always; that truth calmed her anxiety.

She had arranged with the neighbor to watch Doc that day, so after a quick retrieving session outside, she put the dog in his crate.

"You be a good boy, and hopefully I'll be home early enough to go for a jog." She slipped a couple of treats through the grate and left.

No matter how early Miranda walked into the office, her receptionist Rachel was already behind her desk.

"Miranda are you okay?" Rachel asked. "You look …" After a brief pause, she said, "tired."

"You're just being kind. Have you seen the paper yet?" Miranda paused at the receptionist's desk.

"Yes, why?" Rachel asked cautiously.

"Well, I was on the trails. It was my dog and Jake's that found the body. So, yes, you could say my sleep was interrupted last night. You'd think since I was up early enough I would look better. I had plenty of time to cover up with makeup, but you can't really cover up sleep-deprived, swollen eyes. Do I still have a free afternoon?" Miranda leaned against the desk.

"That was you and Jake?" Rachel blurted in astonishment. "And yes, the afternoon is still open. I'll keep it open for you. It won't be too difficult as there are still some appointment openings on Thursdays and Fridays. Can I get some coffee for you?"

"Thanks, Rachel, I could really use another cup. I appreciate it. And when I'm finished for the morning, why don't you put the phones over to the answering service and have an afternoon with those precious girls of yours? You'll still be paid for a full day. You deserve it. Enjoy!" Miranda shuffled toward her office door.

"Wow, really an afternoon off? I think I'd better do some grocery shopping without the girls, and then I can surprise them with a few hours together. Thanks. I'll get your coffee." Rachel shifted out of her seat.

Miranda was studying her files and praying for each client when Rachel walked in with her coffee.

"Mmm, that smells like it will wake me up." Miranda looked up from her desk.

"Were you praying? For your clients?"

"I was. He's the only one who can give me wisdom. How about you Rachel, do you pray?" Miranda held the cup with both hands.

"I do. I thought there was something I felt between us, like a kinship." Rachel smiled and left Miranda to her work.

Miranda stared at Rachel's retreating back. *Thank you, Lord, for answered prayer.* She'd asked for a Christian receptionist.

"By the way." Rachel turned back toward the office. "There were a couple of calls already, a man asking for you. The number was blocked. Do you know who he might be? He wouldn't give me any information even though I tried to get some."

Miranda managed to say, "Thanks, Rachel," before the tingling started and her desk seemed to waver in front of her. She put her hands flat on the desk and took her own oft-offered advice. She breathed in deeply and let it out slowly several times. She wondered again—who could the caller be?

As her vision corrected, there was a knock on the office door and her morning started. It dragged by. The appointments seemed interminable, and it was hard to listen; instead, she found her eyes straying to the clock.

After work, she drove to the police station and found a parking space across the street from it. She dropped her forehead and rested it in her hands, still placed on the steering wheel. *Lord, I'm not strong enough for all this. There has to be a reason someone is hassling me, but what is it? How would he even know I have any tie with Valerie … unless he was at the hospital and had heard me identify Valerie? Lord, I need your strength.*

She bolted upright at the sound of a knock on her window. Her stomach went to her throat as she stared wide-eyed at—Jake. She swung open the door, and before she had a chance to rail at him, Jake folded her in his arms.

"Miranda, I'm sorry I scared you," he whispered.

"I know, but you being sorry doesn't mean I'm not going to tell you off. What do you mean by scaring me? I wasn't even expecting you here. Why are you here?" She finished her tirade still cradled in his arms.

He leaned back and looked down at her. "Well, I was there when you set up a time to come to the station, and I thought you might like some moral support."

"Today I can use the support." She blushed and added, "Would you want to go out to lunch after?" She bit her lip while waiting for his answer.

"I think I can manage to rearrange my schedule. After all, I am the boss and the only employee, for right now that is." Jake grinned, and amber specks twinkled in his deep brown eyes.

Miranda slowly let out her breath. "Well, with that settled, let's go in and get this over with!"

Jake offered his arm as they walked across the street and then he opened the door for Miranda.

"Your mom taught you well. Thank you."

"She did, and I'm glad I can finally use those manners. She told me I'd be glad she taught me well." He faced Miranda. "And you know, she was right." They both chuckled, releasing some of the tension of the day.

"Hello, Miranda," Detective Ryker greeted her. "Jake." The men nodded. "Thanks for coming as promised. Here is the form, and the conference room you can use to fill it out is just over there." He gestured to the far corner.

"Thanks," Jake replied. He took Miranda's arm, and then lead her around the pods of desks, each one scattered with papers, and past a corkboard filled with pictures. Opposite the pods was the dispatch desk heavy with a computer and three monitors. Phones rang, static from the scanner crackled, officers called and shuffled papers, and chairs scraped the floor.

The noise, along with the odors of food and strong coffee, was giving Miranda a headache. She rubbed the bridge of her nose as they entered the conference room. A welcome silence filled the space and with a grateful sigh she sat and read the blank form now set on the table.

It wasn't easy putting everything she'd seen and remembered from the last night on the paper. She still didn't know who the victim was, or who had been calling her name. She peeked at Jake sitting nearby, and he smiled. She felt the rush of heat on her cheeks as she went back to writing. She finally put in the last period and dropped the pen.

"How do you think they work with all that noise going on?" she asked.

"I don't know. I'm with you; I use ear plugs with the noisy machinery." Jake stood. "Finished?"

Miranda nodded and stood. She grabbed the paper, and they made their way back to Nick's temporary desk. She had a few things she wanted to tell the detective in person before they left.

"Thanks, Miranda. How are you after last night?" Nick asked.

"I'm surviving. Do they know who the victim is?"

"Not yet. Do you think you may know who it is?"

"I don't think so but ..." Miranda's face paled, "do you think it could be my sister?"

"I don't think so, but I have a picture of the body if you'd like to see it." Nick's hesitant expression told her that viewing the photograph wouldn't be easy.

Miranda nodded and grabbed Jake's arm, digging her fingers into it for strength.

Nick swiveled his chair, unpinned a picture from a corkboard, and set it on the desk for Miranda to view. She shuddered with sorrow and—relief. It was not Jenny. Wait! She recognized that face! Her head snapped up. "I know that face. I mean I don't know her name, but I've met her before."

"Where?" Nick snapped.

"At … at the Kroger grocery," she stammered.

"Which one?"

"The one by my parents' home." She told him the crossroads. "It's where Valerie used to work."

"Thanks, Miranda. I'll look into it." The detective dismissed them.

Jake put his arm around her shoulders and led her outside. "Let's go to CC's Café. It's pretty close, and we can walk."

Miranda nodded unable to utter a sound. She felt guilty at her relief and mourned the death of the young clerk all at the same time. Maybe those calls were a disgruntled client's spouse after all and had nothing to do with Valerie. But who was the man last night?

Jake hadn't said a word on the way to the restaurant, seeming to understand her need to process what had just happened.

He opened the door, and they stepped into the sweet scent of cinnamon rolls which filled the entry. Jake was a gentleman and seemed to be sensitive to her needs, which was a direct contrast from Derek. He'd talk about himself as if it was the only subject of which he had any knowledge. His model appearance and his solid pursuit of her had blinded her to his ego. Now, she couldn't believe how poor a judge of character she had been. What had he seen in her? She was, after all, normal, not on one extreme or the other in the looks department, which had seemed to matter to him.

"Hi, Jake." The waitress greeted him and wagged her eyebrows. "Your usual table?"

"Hi, Carla, and yes, please. Let me introduce you to Miranda."

"Hi, Carla. It's nice to meet you." Miranda could have sworn Jake had turned red under his beard.

"This way. And to save time, I'll tell you the specials on the way. We have a hot meatloaf sandwich, and the soup of the day is tomato-basil." They were seated in the booth as she finished her recitation, and then she set menus on the table. "What would you like to drink?"

They ordered, and Carla sashayed back to the kitchen.

"Miranda, I'm so sorry you had to experience seeing the picture of the victim and having it be someone you knew. But, isn't it fortunate it wasn't your sister?"

"Jenny's not a victim yet, anyway. Thank you again, Jake. I'm not sure what to say, but I appreciate all you've done for me. However, I think I'm done with hiking for a while. I don't want to find any more bodies." Miranda studied her hands, which were folded in her lap.

"Is that why you declined my dinner invitation? Did you think I was going to ask you to go on another hike?" Jake teased, giving a little chuckle.

"Well, that may have been part of it." She smiled back. "The other part is, I have decided to see if I can visit Valerie." She picked up her menu. "Maybe soon."

"Really? You show more courage than the other women I've known. Just when I think you're going to go home and hide you surprise me. Do you need some company at the hospital?" He covered her hand with his large, warm, rough one.

"Thanks. I keep saying that to you! No, you don't need to come. You have a business and work to do. My afternoon is empty, and I can go to the hospital myself. It will be awkward if her parents are there, but I can handle that. I need to call my mother, too, so she knows I'm all right before the media coverage alerts her to the goings-on. Have you been in touch with your parents?" Miranda let the warmth of his hand radiate strength.

Suddenly, a voice came from nowhere. "What would you two like for lunch?" Both of them jumped at Carla's question.

"I'll have the meatloaf sandwich," Jake announced.

"And I'll have the tomato-basil soup with a side salad and ranch dressing." Miranda smiled trying to cover up her surprise at the waitress's unexpected appearance.

Carla winked and left abruptly.

"She seems … nice," Miranda said.

"She is, and she's also the reason my business has grown so much. She talks it up. I'll bet she could help you get clients, too." He smiled. "Especially since she's seen you with me." Carla returned quickly with lunch interrupting their conversation.

"Oh my, no modesty here." Miranda sipped her soup.

"I only speak the truth." Jake took a bite of his sandwich.

"So what do you have left to do today?" Miranda started on her salad.

"I have a couple more clean-up jobs, and then I'm done for the day. The dinner invitation still stands." He looked hopeful.

"Can I have a raincheck? I'm tired and after the hospital visit, I'm planning to turn in early."

"Sure," he said. They finished eating and soon walked up to the register to pay.

Jake accompanied Miranda to her car and leaned in the open window after she was inside. "Be careful driving. Call if you need to talk." Jake brushed a kiss on her cheek.

"I will on both counts." *You are becoming the man I'd prayed for.* Miranda waved and watched Jake in her rearview mirror until he turned the corner.

CHAPTER FOURTEEN

WEDNESDAY, OCTOBER 23RD

AFTERNOON

The drive from the restaurant to the hospital was uneventful. It was a good thing, too, because Miranda's mind was on the tender kiss and Jake, the kisser. They'd known each other for about four months but in the last four days, she had begun to lose her heart to him. He was in tune to her needs, had impeccable manners, and he could make her laugh. But she couldn't allow herself to fall in love with him until he was on talking terms with God again. *Lord, I don't know Jake's whole story, but you do. Heal his broken spirit and bring him back to you.*

The hospital's parking lot was fairly empty on a Wednesday afternoon, and she slipped the car into a space close to the entrance. Walking down the empty halls, listening to the echo of her heels clicking toward the ICU, it hit her. She was voluntarily putting herself in an emotional storm if Betty Anne and Frank were there, and she'd bet they were already with their daughter.

Steps slowing and shoulders slumping, Miranda realized she was reacting to all the threats from six years earlier. It was time for her to grow up. She straightened and picked up her pace, feeling emotionally stronger already. She had loved Valerie as a sister, and she was willing to see if there was anything she could do to get Betty Anne and her mother back together again as friends.

A man banged through the hospital's swinging doors and in his hurry slammed into her, almost knocking her off her feet. Miranda stared at the swiftly moving man, and a chill raced through. Was there something familiar about him? She shook her head and pushed through those same double doors.

She could smell the fear and feel the hopelessness. She walked past a woman sobbing on a man's chest and noted several people sitting in chairs with their heads bowed as if in prayer.

She located the correct room, and as she entered it, Miranda saw the Clarks before they saw her. She was about to back out when Betty Anne twisted her chair toward the door, and they locked gazes. Immobilized, Miranda was suspended in time. Betty Anne made the first move, a tear seeped out, and she hesitantly raised her arm and took one step, but Frank grabbed her arm. Betty Anne shook loose and moved forward until the two women were wrapped in a hug.

"Betty Anne, I'm so sorry." Miranda's voice croaked with emotion.

"I know," Betty Anne whispered. "Come and sit."

Frank glowered and went to stand at the opposite wall in the small ICU cubicle.

"How is Valerie?" Miranda asked.

"She's hanging on, but they are keeping her in a chemical coma for right now." Betty Anne angled to face Miranda. "They're hoping to bring her out of it tomorrow if she continues to improve. Oh, Miranda, it's been so long. I never imagined this was how we would meet again. I've been praying for you and your family."

"You have?" Miranda didn't mean to sound so abrupt, but the Clarks had sold their house and moved away from their friends without a word.

"I know it didn't seem I cared, but I was so distraught, and Frank thought it best to go and start all over again."

"But how would Valerie have found you if she wanted to." Miranda sat straight with hands in her lap.

"You always were the smart one. I did think about that, so I wrote your mother about a year after we moved, with my new address. She never answered the letter." Betty Anne reached over to cover Miranda's hands.

"Mom never told me you wrote." Miranda didn't think her mother had ever received the letter, or else she certainly would have said something. But as the whole family had been so good at avoiding the subject of Jenny and Valerie, maybe …

"Have you told your mom about Valerie?" Betty Anne asked.

"Well, not yet. I was planning on calling her after my visit here. I couldn't tell her before I knew you had been notified." She had to explain her hesitation to tell her mom.

"Please tell her I miss her and if she can forgive me, I'd like to see her," Betty Anne pleaded.

"I hope you'll forgive me too," Miranda asked.

"Whatever for, dear?"

"Well, I was the last one to see the girls that night they disappeared. If I would have stayed up until Jenny went to bed, they might not have run away." Miranda raised her hands to her face.

"Oh, Miranda there isn't anything to forgive. I never blamed you." Betty Anne leaned over and placed her hands on Miranda's shoulders. "The girls were old enough to take care of themselves. You don't think your mother or I would have left the girls on their own if they needed watching, do you?"

Miranda sensed the question was rhetorical but shook her head.

"Would you like to see Valerie during the next five-minute visit?" Betty Anne dropped her hands and patted Miranda's knee.

"I would if you don't mind. I'd like to pray over her."

"That would be fine. Did you know Valerie was enrolled in college classes?" Before Miranda had a chance to answer Betty Anne went on. "Frank and I plan to visit the college later to see if it would be possible for her to retake the classes without any new charges whenever she is able. We're just not ready to leave her side."

"I can do that for you," Miranda offered without thinking. Should she do it? Well, maybe she could find out which professor taught the botany class Valerie had signed up for. It might help the detective.

"I can't ask you to do that."

"You didn't ask; I offered. I have plenty of time, I'm free all afternoon," Miranda insisted.

"Well, if you insist. I would rather stay here. Frank returns to the hotel to sleep, but I lie down on one of the couches. I can't leave my girl yet. Did you know that Nick Ryker was the detective assigned to the case? Oh, of course you did. He remembered Valerie from high school and has been real supportive." Betty Anne was about to stand, but Miranda stopped her.

"Uh, does Frank still hate me? He didn't look too pleased to see me," Miranda dared to ask in a softer voice.

"No, it's not you. He's got other problems, and this has brought back unwanted memories. He shouldn't take it out on you, though." Both stood, and Betty Anne told the nurse Miranda would be going in to see Valerie.

Miranda walked in the room. Valerie's head was bandaged, and she was hooked up to the monitors, an IV drip taped to her hand. Miranda held Valerie's free hand and prayed for her health, and for the police to find the culprit. When she finished, she brushed a stray lock of hair from Val's forehead. "God be with you," Miranda whispered before leaving the room. Just as she reached the door, the nurse opened it. Miranda hugged Betty Anne and then left the hospital, ready to head to the college.

Driving around the college complex, she read signs to see if she could find the botany department. The college had a modern flare, its slanted roofs shaped like angel wings and its walls filled with windows. It was a small college, so she guessed the sciences were probably combined in one building. Finally, after passing the library, the arts department, the student center, and the mathematics department, she finally found the administrative building.

Miranda didn't want to go back to the visitor parking at the other end of campus, so she drove to find a spot on the street. A car was pulling out, and she was able to parallel park. Summoning her courage, she exited the car and slung her purse on her shoulder then marched across the quiet street and into the building. She heard a buzzing of voices as she progressed down the hall. She glanced at the doors on either side trying to find the administrative office. It seemed unusual to see professors' names on the doors; she'd have thought that their offices would be in their respective departments, not here.

She spotted the registration office and headed toward it. As she did, she passed an office where a heated discussion boomed through the open door. She peeked in the direction of the voices and her eyes locked with the man she'd seen at the grocery store! Her feet were like lead blocks. The blood drained from her face. Her brain finally won, and she moved quickly and dove into the registrar's office.

"You can leave now. I have some business to take care of." The professor gestured to the door, and his visitor left. The professor steepled his fingers and sat back. He'd need to start executing his plan, and soon.

He was tugged out of his concentration by a knock on his door. One of his students stood outside. "Come on in Janet," he said. "How can I help you?"

CHAPTER FIFTEEN

WEDNESDAY, OCTOBER 23RD

EVENING

Jake was tired. He was worn out at the end of this workday, finishing up raking leaves out of the garden. He was weary, too, of resisting his growing feelings for Miranda. He'd thought she'd want his company to see Valerie, but she'd surprised him with renewed inner strength to face another possibly unpleasant situation.

Could he be faithful to one woman? Or was he destined to follow in his father's footsteps and move on when temptation crossed his path? His father had tried reaching out to Jake, but Jake had never returned the calls. Jake's mom had encouraged him to talk with his father. She kept telling him the man had been a good father and Jake had countered, "When he was around, maybe."

Jake still remembered the nights he'd wake up thirsty and on his way for a glass of water, he'd walk by his mom's room, only to hear her quietly sobbing. She hadn't guessed he knew she'd been crying, and he wasn't telling. It surprised him how much it still pained him, as if it had happened only yesterday. Maybe it was true, as his mom had insisted, that she had forgiven her ex-husband with the help of God. Maybe that worked for her, but God hadn't listened to Jake when he was a boy, so why would he listen now?

His cell vibrated in his pocket, and Jake tugged it out to answer. An unknown caller appeared and thinking it could be a new client he answered. "Hello?"

"Is this Jake Stevens?"

"Yes, may I help you?" Jake held the phone to his ear while leaning on the rake.

"I know this is short notice, but I need some clean-up in my yard before Saturday. I'm planning a small party and want the yard to be groomed well enough to make a good first impression. I haven't had time this month to do anything."

"How big is your yard?" Jake thought he could probably do it on Friday afternoon.

"Oh, it's about a quarter acre. I don't think it'll take too much time. I'd appreciate if you could come soon."

"I'll need to meet with you to see what it looks like and give you an estimate. Would you be available right away?"

"I won't be able to go home now, but I'll give you my address, and if you leave your estimate, I'll call you with an okay."

"It's not the way I usually do business."

"I appreciate that, but really need the help. My name is Rodney, and my address is ..." The man rattled off his address. "I'll try to be home tomorrow morning."

"I'll see what I can do." Jake was hesitant.

"Thanks, you're saving me from working in the dark." And then the man hung up.

What a strange call. Jake had had last minute work from new clients before, but someone he knew had always referred them. His business had been built on word of mouth. He had an uneasy feeling about this job ... but why?

Jake pulled up Miranda's contact and pressed it before he could talk himself out of calling, but the phone rolled to voicemail immediately. He hung up, not knowing what to say.

Miranda's first call on her way home was to Detective Ryker. He wasn't in the office, but they gave her the detective's cell phone number. Miranda stopped on the side of the road and dialed. He answered on the second ring.

"Detective Ryker."

"Oh hello, this is Miranda." She was using her Bluetooth and started driving again.

"Miranda, what do you need?"

"I just left the college Valerie attended." It took a moment to gather her thoughts. "I offered to go for the Clarks to see if the college would allow Val to return to her classes once she was well." Oh, she was babbling and not getting to the point.

"That was nice of you. But why are you calling me?"

"Well, remember the voice I heard calling my name Tuesday night? Maybe this doesn't have anything to do with it but …"

"Okay Miranda, get to the point."

"On Sunday I saw a man at the grocery store and um, I was listening in on a conversation. The conversation was between the clerk—the woman who just died, whose body was found—and a man. They were talking about Valerie. Apparently, a professor had invited Val to look at night-blooming flowers, and she had accepted." She fell silent.

"Is that all?" Nick asked.

"No. Today, at the college, I saw the same man I had seen at the grocery store. I asked the administrator how many botany professors held classes, and I was told only two. I don't know if any of it is connected, but thought I should tell you."

"You did the right thing. I'll follow up. Miranda, be careful. Don't go trying to do anything yourself. Okay?"

"I don't think you have to worry about that. If I come across anything else, I'll let you know."

"I'm warning you not to do anything. This guy has killed once and tried once more. He is dangerous, and we don't know what he'll try next."

"Okay." She'd be careful but … she clicked off.

Miranda's next call was to her mother. She punched the speed dial and heard her mom's voice.

"Hello, sweetheart. This is nice to hear from you in the middle of the week."

"Hi, Mom. A testimony to how often I call, huh?"

"It *is* unusual to hear from you in the middle of a work week. So, is something wrong?"

"Yes and no." Miranda pulled to the side of the road. This wasn't going to be an easy conversation.

"Go ahead."

"Mom, do you remember on Sunday that I told you I'd been on that hike? Well, the dogs found a woman that night, a woman who was critically injured. That woman turned out to be Valerie Buchanan." There she'd said it. There was silence on the other end of the line. She should have gone home and told her mom face to face. She was a coward. "Mom, I'm sorry I told you over the phone."

"It's okay, Miranda." Her mom was always able to recover quickly. "Do you know how Valerie is doing?"

"I was just at the hospital and she is in a chemical coma and still in the ICU. From what I understand, they won't know anything until they bring her out of the coma, although I heard she was stable right now. And …"

"And what?"

"I also talked to Betty Anne." The words raced out of her mouth.

"I'm stunned. Did she talk to you? I haven't heard from her since *that day*." Miranda knew which day her mother referred to; no one in the family ever referred to it other than *that day*.

"Really?" Miranda wondered if she should bring up the letter. She'd better, because if her mom went to the hospital, it might come up.

"Really."

"But Betty Anne said she had sent you a letter and never received a reply," Miranda admitted.

"I didn't get the letter." Her mom whispered the words.

"Mom, Betty Anne said she misses you and asked if you would go to the hospital and visit." Miranda's hand and voice shook; she was glad she wasn't driving.

"Are you sure?"

"Uh huh. She is there twenty-four hours a day until Valerie is out of the ICU. I have her cell number if you'd like to call her. She is going to let you decide. Mom, you have to know she welcomed me with open arms. Frank, on the other hand, still seems like he hasn't forgotten."

"I'll have to pray about this, but Miranda I'm proud of you. You've grown into a strong young woman." Her mother hesitated. "Since Jenny's name hasn't come up, does that mean they weren't together when the body was found?"

"Yes," Miranda choked out. "I was hoping Jenny would show up later, but it hasn't happened." A short silence then Miranda murmured, "I'll pray too."

"Thanks, sweetheart. I'll tell you if I go to the hospital."

"Okay, Mom. Bye." Miranda hung and wiped the mist from her eyes before starting for home.

It was 6:00 when Miranda drove into her driveway. Not quite dark yet, but she would still wear her headlamp when she took Doc for a jog; she needed to release some energy. She parked in her driveway, swung out of the car, and then went swiftly up the porch steps and into the house.

"Hey Doc, are you ready for a jog?" she asked, as was her habit. Doc answered with his high-pitched whine. Fifteen minutes later Miranda had shed her work clothes and was ready to go. Both she and Doc donned their reflective vests. It would be dark before they made it home.

Doc led her out the front. Miranda slipped the key into the lock, but before she was finished locking the door, Doc towed her hard to the right side of the house.

"Doc, no," she commanded and countered with a jerk of the leash to the left. The dog reluctantly followed and off they went on their jog. Mr. Anderson was still in his yard and waved as they passed by. He was one of the first neighbors they'd met; his wife brought over a loaf of delicious, moist banana bread right when she'd moved in. Miranda hadn't met many of the other neighbors yet.

The night was clear and she filled her lungs with the cool, fresh air. Her legs pumped in a rhythm with Doc settling in an easy pace. A few cars passed by, but only one of them was polite enough to slow its speed.

While jogging, she cleared her thoughts and as usual, it was a time when she heard God's Word speak to her. A phrase from her previous Bible reading filled her mind. *God is my strength in time of trouble. What does that mean, Lord? I know you are my strength and refuge so does that mean there is trouble coming? Lord, protect us and help Nick find whoever is doing this. Be my mom's strength and encourage her to visit Betty Anne and Valerie.*

Her thoughts drifted to Jake and the two times he'd kissed her. Even though they were brief kisses, she had often felt his protective and gentle reassurance. She sent up a quick prayer. *Lord, bring Jake back into your family.* She'd feel a bit freer to admit her attraction to him then, that is if he felt the same way about her. She had the distinct impression he did.

They'd finished the three miles and slowed for the last two blocks. A car was heading toward them with its bright lights beaming. There weren't any sidewalks but there was a driveway up ahead, and she thought they could make it before the car reached them. Otherwise, they could step into the shallow ditch to be safe. Miranda picked up the pace, but at the same time, the car increased speed. The driver had to see them; they were wearing reflective vests! Miranda started jogging and then running but the car seemed to want to beat her to the driveway. She heard the power of the car. It was heading right for them! Doc jerked the leash and Miranda went head-first into the ditch. Brambles caught the side of her face; the barbs sliced her cheek, and she felt a pop in her ankle, followed by a sharp pain. Still, she hung on to Doc's leash as he continued to drag her further into the ditch.

She lifted her head just in time to see the car swing its front end back toward the center of the street. She shivered at the realization it was the same car that had passed them earlier. The only vehicle to slow as it had passed by.

Miranda jumped up to memorize the license plate number but quickly crumpled in pain. Doc sidled up next to her and whined. She patted his head, and he licked her face, but she pushed him away to stop the sting from the brambles. Each lick felt as though a thorn was being pushed deeper into the soft tissue. "Well, we got out of the way from that one," she reassured him. "What a reckless driver. I was hoping to turn him in."

Mr. Johnson was at her side before she had a chance to call anyone. "Miranda, are you okay? I saw that car almost hit you. Oh! Your face, my dear. Let's get you back and I'll have the missus clean it for you."

"I think I can take care of it. But thanks." She had an important question to ask him. "You didn't get the license plate number did you?" Miranda rubbed her ankle.

"No, but are you okay?"

"I twisted my ankle, too. Let's see if I can stand." She took Mr. Johnson's hand and slowly put weight on her left ankle. It hurt, but she thought she'd be able to make it home. Then ice and a wrap. "I think I can manage. Thanks for your help."

He helped her most of the way, but Miranda insisted she could make it home to take care of the scratches. "Thanks again, Mr. Johnson."

"Call if you need any help."

"I will."

Hobbling to her house, she grabbed the rail and hefted herself up the steps and stilled—puzzled at the debris scattered on the porch floor. She picked up a piece of whatever had been scattered. A black petal. She looked around. It was as if someone had plucked the petals off of a dozen flowers. Black flowers! She needed to call Jake. He knew flowers maybe he could help her out.

CHAPTER SIXTEEN

WEDNESDAY, OCTOBER 23RD

NIGHTTIME

Miranda hadn't dressed for the drop in temperature. And she hadn't planned on having to sit on her porch after she finished her jog. Relief overwhelmed her when Jake answered on the first ring and told her he was on his way.

She shivered from the cold even with Doc glued to her side. Her ankle ached and her face stung. Who had been driving the car, a car that had unmistakably aimed for her? Who could have left the petals, and was this a coincidence? She'd never seen black flowers before. The man who had told Valerie about the night-blooming flowers was a botany professor if he'd been telling the truth. Could he be the man behind this? Maybe she was jumping to conclusions.

Jake's red Dodge stopped in front of her house. He threw open the door, slammed it shut, and charged toward Miranda. She stood, and Jake folded her tightly to him. She clung to his jacket and buried her face in his solid chest, and when she did, her worries seemed to fade away. She didn't want to think anymore. A crunch of tires slowing in front of the house sounded, but Miranda was reluctant to release Jake.

"I called Nick because there are a few different meanings behind black roses. None of them good," Jake whispered. He leaned back to see Miranda and gasped. "Miranda, you didn't tell me about your face. We need to take care of that soon."

"I can take care of the scratches when I can enter my house." She had a more pressing question. "What do black roses mean?" She met his eyes, fear in her voice.

Jake sighed before answering. "Revenge or death would be my guess. If you were into gothic or a lot of black, then the bouquets would be welcome. But you're not." He slowly released her from the hug, but entwined his fingers with hers.

Miranda couldn't believe this was happening to her in this small, safe town. Gaining strength from Jake's grasp, she stood a little straighter to meet Nick; she couldn't let herself crumble in front of the detective.

"Miranda." Nick greeted her and then cringed at the sight of her face. "What happened?"

She swallowed back the lump in her throat and allowed her anger a vent. How could someone act so mercilessly to another person? She proceeded to tell the detective about the anonymous calls as well as that night's incident. "How could anyone even do such a thing?" Miranda clenched her free fist, digging her nails into her palm.

"We don't know yet, but you've given us something to check out. Why didn't you mention the calls when you were down at the station?"

"I thought they were probably from a disgruntled client's husband. I've never had one before, but I supposed it could happen. Maybe *all* of this is from a disgruntled client." She clung tighter to Jake's hand.

"I see. Could you give us a list of any possible clients? We will check out the professors, too."

"I wouldn't even know who or why. I just thought you ought to be aware of the possibility." Miranda couldn't release any names of her clients or their families as possible suspects; nothing had actually happened yet, and she had her own code of confidentiality.

"Can you think of anything else that happened tonight? Anything unusual at all?"

Miranda thought for a moment and slowly nodded. "Yesss," she dragged out the word. "As I was locking up the door on our way out for a jog, Doc jerked me to the right side of the house." She pointed in the direction. Then she started moving in that direction, dragging Jake and Doc with her.

"Wait here. Let us check it out," Nick ordered and proceeded to choose a couple of deputies Miranda didn't recognize to search the area.

"Detective!" One of the men soon shouted. "You will want to see this."

Nick clicked on his flashlight and disappeared around the side of the house.

"What did they find?" Miranda asked, not expecting an answer.

"Wait. Nick will come back and tell us what's going on." Jake let go of her hand and snaked his arm around her shoulders. In the meantime, I think I will be sleeping on your couch for a few nights until all this is sorted out."

"That's not necessary. I have Doc. He's a good watchdog, and I'll call 911. I just need to let him be the guard dog he wants to be and trust his instincts." *But if anything ever happened to him, I wouldn't be able to forgive myself.*

Nick emerged from the side of the house carrying an evidence bag and heading straight for his car.

Miranda peered up questioningly at Jake, but he shrugged his shoulders and mouthed, *Wait.* Waiting might be easy for Jake, but she wanted to know what was going on! She disengaged from Jake and headed, limping, toward the detective, Doc following on leash. Her ankle wouldn't quit throbbing. Jake caught up in three strides and followed.

"What did you find?" Miranda closed in on the detective at his car.

Nick shot a glance at the pair and sighed. "We found more rose petals."

"So he *was* on the side of my house. I should have let Doc go there and then I could have called 911, and this would all be over." She felt like a fool.

"You did the right thing. I wouldn't have wanted you to find this guy. Remember, if it's the same guy, he's already killed one woman and almost succeeded with Valerie." She saw the anxiety in Nick's eyes when he mentioned Val.

At one time she'd heard from her sister that Nick and Valerie had spent a lot of time together. But Nick was a Christian and was always proselytizing so Valerie would listen to him. Valerie had told Jenny, "Nick is so good looking that I can turn my ears off and my eyes on."

Miranda suspected Nick still was attracted to Valerie. And what man wouldn't be attracted to the tall, slender blonde?

"Nick, do you think it's a good idea if I stay at Miranda's for a few days?" Jake appealed to the higher authority, trying to overturn Miranda's decision.

"It probably wouldn't hurt …"

"See, Miranda? I will be staying." Jake gave her a firm nod.

"Jake," Nick continued, "you didn't let me finish. I'm going to make sure we have a deputy drive by every hour. With her dog, I think she'll be fine."

Miranda agreed. "Jake, I appreciate the offer, but I think Doc and I will be fine. Go home and sleep. If I can't sleep, I'll call you. Okay? I promise I will keep all the doors and windows locked and if Doc barks I'll call you. With the deputies driving by, someone will always be close." Miranda reassured Jake, her eyes staring into his unsure brown pools.

"Okay," he conceded grudgingly.

"Now that's all settled, I'm heading to the office. Unfortunately, the ground is hard, and there weren't any footprints. The petals are the only evidence that someone was there. I'll be in touch." Nick climbed into his car as did the deputies, and they all drove off.

Jake followed Miranda toward the front door, helping her up the steps.

"Would you like to come in for some hot chocolate? I'm freezing and need something warm. The company would be appreciated." Miranda smiled up at him then turned back to unlock the house.

126

"I'll take you up on that offer." Jake followed Miranda in the house and down the hall to the kitchen.

Miranda filled a pan with milk to heat on the stove. Then she pulled out the chocolate syrup and squirted in a big helping. He noticed how she was making the drinks. "Wow, we're not doing the powder stuff? Do you have marshmallows?"

"Better than marshmallows I have whipped cream. I'm in a mood for real hot chocolate." As it simmered, she let Jake clean up her face, flinching each time he pulled out a barb.

"You're all cleaned up."

"Jake, thanks for coming so quick. I don't know what I would have done if you hadn't answered my call." Her eyes felt misty at the confession.

"Miranda, I care for you and will come anytime you need me." Jake stood and closed the gap, embracing Miranda's trembling body.

Miranda tilted her head up and saw the deep emotion held in his eyes as he lowered his head and just before their lips met she whispered, "I care for you too." And she did. She felt protected and as the kiss deepened she answered his longing with a longing of her own.

Jake broke off the kiss and Miranda, breathless, peered up at him.

"I'm not sorry that happened." He brushed her forehead with his lips.

"I'm not either." Maybe she shouldn't have let that happen, but she had no guilt whatsoever. "Now you see why I can't let you stay." She tried for a light teasing tone even though she was serious. She saw steam rise from the stovetop. "Oh no, move over or we won't have hot chocolate." Miranda pushed Jake out her way and grabbed the wooden spoon, then started stirring the hot chocolate. "Whew, just in time. Could you get the can of whipped cream from the fridge?"

Jake went to the fridge, found the can, and started shaking it. "Are you ready for it?"

Miranda poured two mugs of the steamy, sweet brew and Jake topped them off with whipped cream.

They sat at the table and talked about their respective childhoods and found they had a lot in common. The only thing they didn't have in common was a history of hiking. And Miranda didn't want to go out on the trail again anytime soon. Maybe next summer. That would be soon enough.

Jake looked at his watch, and his eyes widened.

"What?" Miranda asked picking up the empty cups to put in the dishwasher.

"I've been here for over two hours and would love to spend more time, but I have a full day tomorrow. Are you sure I can't have your couch tonight?" he teased.

She looked at him in mock horror. "No, sir." She grasped his arm and tugged him down the hall.

"Okay, okay. I'll leave but not before this." Jake bent his head and tenderly kissed her once more. "Good night. Oh, and how about lunch tomorrow? We can go to CC's and hear the new gossip."

Miranda opened the door. "I'd like to go to lunch." Then she urged him out the door. "Good night, Jake." She waved and then she slowly closed and locked the door. She believed she would sleep well.

He was going to have to move quickly now that things were falling into place. He watched the red truck leave, rolling slowly from the curb. She was scared—he could almost smell the fear. He thought it funny that the boyfriend had been the first to show up, even before the police.

Miranda probably still doesn't know who is behind it all. She hadn't known he had been the rude man who'd run into her at the hospital when she'd visited Valerie. He'd learned Valerie was still alive, then, and that Valerie's parents were at the hospital, too. He hated to disappoint parents. With them at the hospital, he'd have to be more careful in finishing her off, but he could do it.

As for his other victim, he'd actually felt justified in ending his stepbrother's life, devastating his stepmother's remaining years. She'd devastated his life, after all.

Those two, stepmother and stepbrother, had invaded his life alone with his father. Of course, his father had been elated and had spent most of his time with—them. There was one upside, though; he had to admit his father no longer pestered *him* anymore. That was the *only* bright side. The last time he'd seen his stepmother was after his father had died. She'd tried to invite him over for holidays afterward, but he always turned her down without excuse. She finally stopped asking and that had been that.

Then Jared entered his life again, so proud that he had finally broken his drug habit and was ready to expose his dealer. Well, little stepbrother, I guess you broke the drug habit, but you didn't expose anyone.

He slowly drove away, satisfied Miranda was scared. He had more to come.

CHAPTER SEVENTEEN

THURSDAY, OCTOBER 24TH

MORNING

Jake had finished raking the leaves and piled them in the garbage cans. His face heated in spite of the cool breeze as he remembered last night's kiss. And, wow, she had kissed him back. Miranda was smart, a great listener, and yet vulnerable. He wanted to shield her from anything else bad. *Well, God, if you are out there, why would you let stuff like this happen to Miranda? She doesn't deserve any of this, and neither did my mom when my dad walked out on us. What kind of a God lets these things happen?*

He hadn't been able to reconcile a loving God who is supposed to answer prayers with the wickedness that people can do to one another. He shook those thoughts out of his mind and lifted the cans into the back of his truck and whistled for Katie.

The little black lab raced toward him and leapt in the open door. "Good girl."

Jake climbed in and started the truck. He was on his way to check out tomorrow's new job with Mr. Green. It was about a 45-minute drive, but if Jake remembered the neighborhood, it was a nice one, and he could get some new clients .

He drove down the street looking for the right address and stopped in front of a white stucco rambler with almost-black wood trim. Jake opened his door and stepped down, stopping Katie as she tried to bolt out.

"No girl. You stay in the truck. Not everybody wants a dog running in his or her yard. And this yard looks like it's owned by one of those kinds of people."

Jake noticed the perfect cut of the murraya hedge and could imagine its orange-blossom scent when it flowered. There was a break in the hedge for a sidewalk, one that lead to the front door. Walking down the sidewalk, Jake noticed a garden of pruned rose plants without their late-autumn blooms; opposite were fading hydrangeas. Along the front of the house were azalea plants. There was an impressive magnolia tree on a grass patch which had been groomed to look like a golf course on one side of the front yard and a Japanese maple tree on the other side. On one side of the house was a large maple tree stripped of its leaves for autumn. It would shade the house in the summer. It was extraordinary and looked perfectly groomed. He puzzled over why he had been called.

He continued to the house and rang the bell. Jake waited, and after a couple of minutes tried again. Still no answer, so he knocked loudly. Where was Mr. Green? Jake decided to go around to the backyard. Ah—this is what Mr. Green wanted to be cleaned up. The back was the direct opposite of the front yard. Weeds filled the flower beds and leaves covered the backyard. The backyard was less than a quarter of an acre, and Jake estimated he would probably be done in about three hours. Long enough to do a thorough job.

Jake called Mr. Green to find out why he hadn't made it home only to get his voicemail. He left a message. Well, if the guy called back he could still refuse to take the job, but the chance to gain a foothold in this neighborhood was tempting.

Jake continued to look around. A large greenhouse stood in the back corner of the yard, a burn barrel about ten feet in front of it, and he started to walk toward it when the sudden sound of barking stopped him in his tracks. He sprinted to the front of the house. Why would Katie bark? He didn't want her disturbing the neighbors. As he rounded the corner, he caught sight of a tall man with close-cropped hair coming toward him.

"Hello." Jake waved at the stranger. "Are you Mr. Green?"

"Yes, I am," said the man. He looked to be in his forties.

"I hope you don't mind my looking around at the back. When I saw the front yard, I wondered why you needed my help."

"Oh, that's okay." He waved his hand in dismissal. "Do you think you could get the work done in an afternoon?"

"I can get a lot of it done so it will look presentable for your guests in the evening. It would take more than a few hours to shape it up, but if the guests are only going to look at it from inside the house, one afternoon should be sufficient." Jake stuffed his hands in his pockets. "If you'd still like me to do the work I can get a contract from the truck."

"Yes, yes. I want you to do the work. I'm in class during the afternoon. Do I need to be here while you do the clean-up?" He kept pace with Jake as they strode to the truck. Katie started barking once more.

"Calm down, girl. We'll be going soon." Jake climbed in the cab, reached over the seat for his briefcase, and pulled out a clipboard with the contract attached.

"I charge $100.00 for the first hour and $75.00 each hour after that. I estimate this will take me about three hours. Are you still interested?" Jake handed over the clipboard.

"That sounds reasonable to me. Do you like to be paid in advance?"

"Yes, with first-time clients. You can leave the payment in an envelope under the front doormat. If it's there, I'll do the work and if not, I'll assume you decided not to go ahead with the project."

"You are reasonable. Where do I sign?"

Jake handed a pen to Mr. Green and pointed to the signature line. Mr. Green signed and returned the clipboard. "I'll be here tomorrow afternoon then," Jake said. "You have my number in case there are any changes."

"I don't think there will be any changes. Thanks." Mr. Green held out his hand, and they shook. "I need to get back to work."

"Thank you." Jake climbed back in his truck and settled down Katie, who was growling under her breath, and drove off to meet Miranda for lunch.

"Everything is set for tomorrow, sir." The man held a cellphone to his ear.

"Good. Did Jake believe you were me?" the professor asked.

"Yes. He's planning on being there in the afternoon. He'd like an envelope with payment or he won't do the work."

"That's not a problem. How much?" Jake was playing right into his hands. The man told him the quote. The professor had been willing to give him much more than quoted. Hmm, maybe he would put extra in the envelope. After all, Jake wouldn't be done as soon as he thought he would. "Okay. Are you all set for tomorrow? You have the key?"

"Of course. I'm a detailed person. I think of all possibilities, and this will be easier than most jobs. I'll expect an envelope tomorrow, too."

"You'll get it. Half then and half after, as agreed." All the pieces of the puzzle were falling into place.

Miranda paced away from her desk, around the office chairs, and then back to her desk again. She looked at the plants, but they were doing fine—they didn't even have any dead leaves she could pluck off. Tired of the pacing she walked out to the reception area and faced Rachel.

"Any word from Jake?" she asked for the tenth time.

"No. You're as bad as one of my girls asking, 'Are we there yet?'" Rachel grinned with amusement.

"Well, he's late, and I have an afternoon appointment." After that last kiss, she was looking forward to seeing him. Really looking forward to it. She hadn't been able to keep still all morning. Between appointments, she relived their moments together and wondered if Jake felt the same way she did. "Are you going to have lunch with your girls today?"

"Yeah. They like it when I come to school, so I try to go as often as possible. Did you need me to stay in the office today?" There was hesitation in her voice as if she wasn't sure if she should take off for lunch.

"Hey, it's not a problem. Why don't you leave now? And say 'hi' to the girls for me. One of these days we need to be formally introduced. Have fun. I can wait alone for Jake." She'd been alone for the last six months, after all, and then Jake decided it was time to see if there was something more than being acquaintances. She could hardly wait to see him.

"If you're sure, I will take off now." Rachel reached down to pull out her purse and stood. "Thanks, Miranda." She pranced out as happy as a child.

A moment later Jake appeared in the doorway, grinning from ear to ear.

"Hello." He'd managed to look devastatingly handsome even in his work clothes. His jacket loosely covered his broad chest and his work pants fit snug to his narrow hips and hung loosely around what she figured were muscular thighs.

"Hello, yourself. Do I have something stuck in my beard? You're staring." He stepped up in front of her and held out his hands. She slid hers into his, and he curled his fingers around then tugged her up from the chair. He pulled her in a hug and brushed his lips against her forehead. "Ready for lunch?"

"I'm starved." She pulled away and moved toward the door; if she didn't, she might just stay in his arms and not eat lunch at all. "Let's go! Maybe we'll hear some news at CC's." She gave him a teasing grin.

Jake followed, and when they stepped on the sidewalk, he drew her arm through his. She felt the strength of his arm. His warmth eased some of the sense of malevolence she'd been feeling in the past twenty-four hours. Jake's light heartedness helped her refocus.

"You're in a good mood this afternoon. Mind telling me why?"

"Well, I landed a job in a neighborhood I've been trying to break into for a while now. The house belongs to a professor. Apparently, his usual guy was sick, and he'd heard about my work, so he called."

Miranda stiffened at the word "professor." Hadn't Jake been listening to everything she'd told Nick the other night? They were checking out the botany professors at the college. "Did you meet him?"

"Yes, a nice man and very agreeable. I'll do a clean-up job tomorrow afternoon." They reached the café and Jake opened the door.

"Hi, you two. A table in a quiet corner?" Carla winked. "I have just the place. Follow me." Both Miranda's and Jake's face flamed. Miranda took a deep breath, trying to calm her anxiety by taking in the delicious aroma of fried chicken. She didn't like to be the center of attention and didn't want this new relationship to be the talk of the town, but in a small town, what could she expect?

Carla seated the couple and placed menus on the table and—surprisingly—without a word, left.

"She didn't say anything else?"

"No." Jake smiled. "She surprises me sometimes with her silence, but she does know most people's business and usually isn't afraid to pass on pertinent information."

Miranda's stomach grumbled, and she looked up and locked eyes with Jake. They burst out laughing; he must have heard it, too.

Jake ordered the fried chicken with mashed potatoes and a vegetable and Miranda ordered an Asian salad. Over lunch, they continued to talk about their childhoods and favorite school subjects and sports. She laughed at his antics in school, things she wouldn't dream of doing. Miranda was surprised to learn Jake didn't watch many sports, but he enjoyed watching the Olympics. She did, too.

Lunch was finished all too soon, and as Jake escorted her back to her office, she felt a strange sensation of tension growing. She was confused why she should feel any tension at all. Miranda saw Rachel ahead and called to her.

"Rachel, wait up. I'll follow you into the office." She turned to Jake. "Thanks for a great lunch. I see your truck across the street. I'll just catch up to Rachel, and you can get back to work." She reached up and pecked his cheek then walked fast to catch up with Rachel. Before entering the building, she turned and waved at Jake, and he waved back.

Miranda slid her key into the lock and entered the office first. She took a few steps then stopped abruptly and lurched forward. Rachel slammed into her back. The trembling started in her cheeks, her hands shook, and her knees felt wobbly.

"What is all this?" Rachel cried.

"Call 911," Miranda's shaky voice mumbled. "We need Nick."

In spite of the fact that the door had been locked, there on the floor outside her inner office door laid a wilting bouquet of black roses. Miranda felt lightheaded, and she backed up into one of the reception chairs. *Why is this happening, Lord? Who is targeting me? I'm weary of the whole thing. I need your strength to continue and faith that you will protect me.*

CHAPTER EIGHTEEN

THURSDAY, OCTOBER 24TH

AFTERNOON

Nick swung open the office door and entered, followed by Deputy Pete Sweete and a crime tech Miranda had seen at her house the night before.

"Here we are again," she said. "Whoever this is knows where I live and where I work." Miranda sat in one of the chairs across from her office door staring at the black bouquet propped against it.

Nick sat next to Miranda while the tech went to work. "I think you may want to take Jake up on his offer from last night. In the meantime, the tech will need fingerprints from both you and Rachel for elimination. We may get lucky and get a print, but it's more likely this person wore gloves."

"I called Jake," she said. "He'll be here to pick me up at the end of the day, and I have Doc, of course."

"Do you know any of the other tenants in the building?" Nick pulled out a small notepad and pen.

"Other than speaking an infrequent 'good morning,' I haven't met anyone from the escrow company across the hall or the architect at the end of the hall. It's pretty quiet around here. And the door was locked; I had to use my key to get in. I just don't understand—how could someone get inside? There aren't any windows low enough to climb through."

"It's one of the things we'll be looking for, to see if there are any signs of forcing the lock. Is the landlord easy to contact? He or she may be a big help."

Miranda stood to go to Rachel's desk, where Rachel sat. She handed a business card to Miranda, and Miranda smiled her thanks.

"Here, he's been very helpful." She handed the card to Nick. "How much longer before you're done?" Miranda watched the work. They'd already bagged the bouquet, and she was glad not to have to see the thing any longer. She shivered at the memory of it.

"Can you cancel your next appointment? This takes a little time."

"Okay." Miranda looked to Rachel, who had already picked up the phone to try and reach the client before she left home.

The office door opened again, and Anne charged into the office. She stopped and looked around until she caught sight of Miranda. Then, Anne rushed over and bent to hug Miranda. Miranda clung to Anne, having to swallow back the lump in her throat.

"Anne, what are you doing here?" Miranda released her friend.

"Jake called and was worried about you. I told him I'd come right over." Anne stood and stared at Nick. "Hi, Nick. I read in the paper you were heading up the investigation. So—do you think it's just one person or more than one person?"

"Anne, nice to see you too. If you've read the paper, you know everything." Nick stood. "I'll be in touch. In the meantime Miranda, be careful and have someone with you wherever you go. We'll continue to keep the hourly watch on your house." He left the office.

Pete Sweete ambled over and pulled out a pad and pen from his hip pocket. Miranda wondered what he wanted because Nick was in charge of this investigation and had already left. Anne rolled her eyes.

"Well, Miranda, where was Jake this afternoon?"

Miranda's brows furrowed. "Why?"

"We need to know where everyone was to eliminate suspects. He was there when both the victims were found, and he could have planted the flowers at your house. Now, where was he?"

"Pete." He startled as Anne spoke. "Nick is the head of this investigation. I think he would have asked that question if it was relevant." They stared at one another.

"Anne, it's okay," Miranda spoke up. "Jake was with me for lunch and left me at the outside door to the building."

Anne leaned in and whispered in Miranda's ear. "Notice how he waited until Nick left. He's not in charge. My guess is he wants to catch Jake doing something for which he can arrest him. You don't have to answer his questions."

Miranda's eyes widened.

"What are you whispering about?" The deputy glowered.

"I'm just making sure Miranda knows her rights." Anne's round eyes feigned innocence.

"I'm done." The tech spoke up and moved next to Pete. He had his arms full. "Could you pick up the rest for me, deputy? Thanks." The tech nodded his head in the direction of the equipment. "You can have your office back," he said to me.

"Thanks." Miranda stood and held the door open for the men. After they had left, she turned back to Anne. "What's this about Jake and Pete?"

Anne chuckled. "Pete thinks any man who has long hair and a beard has something to hide. He's been looking for something to hold against Jake. It's a small town, so the news gets around."

"How could anyone think that of Jake? He's perceptive, thoughtful, courageous, and has a great sense of humor. I haven't seen anything that's inconsistent with those character traits, or anything to raise a red flag."

"Hey, I agree. I'm just telling you how Pete Sweete thinks. So you and Jake, huh?" She raised her eyebrows.

"Um, well we are getting to know each other better." Miranda couldn't hide her blush.

"He's a nice guy, but be careful. Will you be all right now? I have a little boy about to get home from school." Anne stood.

"I think Rachel and I will be fine." Miranda stood, too, and hugged Anne. "Thanks for coming."

"See you Sunday morning?"

"You bet. See you then." Miranda strolled past Rachel's desk to her office. "Thanks, Rachel."

"Ahhh … Miranda?" Rachel's hesitant voice stopped Miranda, and she turned.

"Yes?"

"I was wondering if I might leave a little early tomorrow? My oldest daughter has a dental appointment. But with everything that's going on, I could reschedule if you need me here," Rachel rushed to add.

"Don't worry. Go ahead and keep the appointment. I'll be okay. Jake will probably pick me up, and we'll make sure the door is locked. And I'll have Doc with me." Miranda entered her office and sat behind her desk, picking up the file for her next appointment.

The afternoon whizzed by and at the end of it, Miranda jolted from studying the next days' client files when she heard a knock on her door.

"Miranda, it's 5:00 and I'm leaving. Jake is in the waiting area." Rachel popped into the room.

"Okay. I'll see you in the morning. Jake can come in the office."

Rachel bobbed her head and left.

"Hi." Jake smiled as he strode to her desk. "How about I take you out to dinner?"

"Jake, I'm too tired to go out. Would it be okay if we picked up teriyaki and ate at my house? Then Doc and Katie could play in the backyard for a while." Miranda rubbed her temples to ease the ache.

"That's fine. I want to follow you. Let's call ahead so I just have to run into the restaurant for a minute." Jake pulled out his phone, looked up the restaurant's number, and called. "It'll be ready in twenty minutes. Are you ready now?"

Miranda straightened her desk and stood. She walked to the plants and checked the soil. It was still moist. No need to water these plants that didn't mind being neglected!

She looked up as Jake held out her coat. He was a gentleman. Who did Pete think he was, trying to find something against Jake? She shrugged into her coat, and they left the office. Jake's warm touch on her back guided the way. After locking the door, they quickly scrambled down the steps and into their respective vehicles.

The professor watched from his car as the two left the office and climbed into their vehicles. Neither seemed to notice he'd been sitting there for the last few hours. He needed to blend in with the rest of the cars on the road. Renting this common model and color had been a brilliant move.

She has her dog with her so he'd have to find a way to silence the mutt. He'd already taken steps to get Jake out of the way.

They think the hourly drive-by the police are doing around her house will keep her safe. He'd found out about that while he had her home under surveillance the night before. No, he'd make his move in a public place and soon. She was sufficiently scared now, and he wanted to add just a little more fear. *Wait until she gets home.* A malicious chuckle erupted.

He'd ticked off the possible problems and was about to finish up in a couple of days. He checked them off in his head. *Jared, who started this whole ordeal—gone. His girlfriend, encouraging Jared— she'd be gone in two days. The clerk who could identify him—gone. And now, Miranda, who knows me but doesn't know me. I have a special plan for the meddling busybody, and then she, too, will be—gone. No one left to identify me. List finished.*

Miranda drove into her driveway, and Jake parked his truck in front of her house. Jake took the food and his backpack with him; he and Katie met Miranda and Doc on the porch. Miranda unlocked the door, and they all entered. The dogs took off down the hall and the telltale bang at the kitchen door, Miranda knew Doc had slid across the floor in his enthusiasm. The corners of her mouth twitched at the dog's antics.

"That dog of mine. I think he remembers to stop too late. Will you let them out? I'm going back out to get the mail." Miranda turned to go but was stopped by a strong grip on her arm.

"Oh no, you don't. We'll go both together." Jake held tight until she complied.

"Okay. But I don't see why. The dogs don't seem to have noticed anything unusual."

Jake shook his head. "We can't be too careful."

"Okay," she said grudgingly.

The dogs happily chased one another around the yard while Miranda led the way to the mailbox. She reached inside and then quickly snatched her hand out as if she had been stung. She brought her finger to her mouth. What pricked her?

"Miranda let me see." Jake held her to him and with his free hand plucked out his keys and used the small attached flashlight to see what was inside the mailbox. "We need to call Nick," he said.

"What is it?" Miranda trembled. "If it's another black rose, we know there probably aren't any fingerprints," she said wearily. "Let's take a look at it first." Miranda reached in front of Jake and drew out the mailbox's contents.

Another black rose—but, this time, a note was attached. In bold print, it read,

Miranda! I'll see you soon!

Her legs wobbled; if not for Jake holding her up she'd be sitting on the sidewalk. *Who is this, Lord?*

"Okay, call Nick," she agreed.

It didn't take long for Nick to arrive, alone this time. He bagged the rose and note. And with the assurance he would have some officers walking by her office regularly tomorrow, too, he left.

"Come on Miranda. Let's go heat up dinner." Jake put his arm around her waist to support her on the way to the house.

"I'm not hungry." Miranda let Jake help her into the house.

"I am, and I want you to know I'm a light sleeper. I won't let anything happen to you tonight." Jake put the food on a plate and placed it in the microwave.

"Jake, could this be that professor I saw on Sunday? He is the same guy I saw at the college, and when we locked eyes, it was almost as if he was challenging me." Miranda sat with elbows on the table and head in her hands.

"I don't know." He set the first plate in front of Miranda along with a fork. "On the one hand, a botany professor would probably know about flowers. But why would a professor want to kill a couple of unrelated women?" He put another plate in the microwave.

"Well, most serial killers seem like normal people. But I think the two were related somehow. The only reason I can come up with is that both Valerie and the clerk worked at the same store. And what about the car that slowed down? I'm pretty sure it was the same car that ran me off the side of the road while I was jogging with Doc. But that was such a common-looking car. I saw one just like it parked by the office most of today and I've seen the same model and color in other places too." Miranda picked up her fork. She should attempt a bite or two after Jake took the trouble to warm it up. "I guess the biggest problem I have is—why me? What is the common denominator?"

"Well, if it is the man you saw in the grocery store," Jake mused thoughtfully, "he might think you overheard something important. Did he say much?"

"Hardly anything. He just said the clerk must be mistaken, that he was certainly not the person she'd seen with Valerie. When I talked with her, she was excited to see the night-blooming flowers. I told her to call me if she found them and gave her my ..." Miranda dropped her head in her hands.

"What?"

"I gave her my card. Do you think whoever murdered her has my card? No. When I get someone's card, I put it in my desk or in my purse." Miranda shook her head. "But that doesn't mean everyone does. I don't know. Let's talk about something else."

"Okay. There's a highly-rated action thriller movie showing. How about a movie tomorrow night?" Jake's grin widened.

"Oh no," Miranda groaned. "I think a comedy is in order. I don't want to remind myself of the past few days. We've been living in our *own* thriller."

"All right, a comedy it is. What are your all-time favorite movies?"

"Really?" At Jake's nod she answered. "*Pride and Prejudice*, and after that I like musicals. How about you? Oh, let me guess. Action thrillers?"

"How did you guess?" His teasing grin spread. "But I have to say, being raised by my mom I watched my share of musicals, and I enjoyed them. I'd rather go to the theater to see them, though, and watch the actors on stage."

"Same here." Then she grew serious. "Jake, are you planning on staying here tonight?"

"Yes, but don't worry. I will be on the couch." He'd read her mind.

"I'm not worried about you; it's others that will talk about it. But I don't see any other way to feel even a little safe. I appreciate you doing this."

"It was gossip that drove me away from church," Jake admitted. "I will explain the truth if anyone even hints at anything other than what is truly going on, Miranda. Don't worry." Jake covered her hands with his and looked into her eyes. She thought he might kiss her, and she wanted him to, but she resisted and pulled her hands away.

"Thanks. I wish it were that easy. Anyway, the people who count will know what's going on. Now it's time for bed. Will you get the dogs? They're probably hungry. I'll get bedding and a pillow for you." Miranda headed upstairs. Sometime soon she wanted to find out what Jake had experienced that had caused the rift between him and God. But first, they both needed to sleep.

What was tomorrow going to bring?

CHAPTER NINETEEN

FRIDAY, OCTOBER 25TH

Miranda woke up to the aroma of strong coffee drifting into her bedroom. And—something that smelled like pancakes. Then, she heard a faint sound of sizzling. Pulling back the covers, she slipped her legs over the side of her bed, drew her arms into her robe, and slid into her slippers. She hurried down to the kitchen, hardly noticing any pain in her ankle.

Wow! A man was cooking in her kitchen. Derek, the former boyfriend, had always expected *her* to cook. He hadn't lifted a finger in the kitchen, not even to help with dishes.

"Morning. Mmm … it smells delicious." Miranda licked her lips in anticipation. "Did you learn to cook from fear of starvation? Or did you get tired of frozen meals?" she teased, pouring two mugs of coffee and setting them on the table before sitting down herself.

"Ha-ha. Mom taught me to cook. She said all the women would flock around me if I could cook. Since it was just the two of us, I learned some of the domestic skills, and she tried her best to let me be a boy and grow into a man. She had the patience of Job, as the saying goes, and didn't let me quit even when I burned the food." Jake flipped the last pancake onto the plate and set it in the middle of the already-set table. He then sat opposite Miranda.

"Do you mind if I pray?" Miranda folded her hands and, at Jake's nod, she bowed her head. "Lord, thanks for Jake's skill as a cook and for the food you provide. Bless our bodies with it. Please give us wisdom in all our decisions with all the incidents that seem to be threatening us. Be with Valerie as she recovers and her parents as they knit their family back together. And if Jenny is out there, please return her home safely. Amen." Miranda picked up her fork and stabbed a pancake.

"Do you really believe that God will answer all your prayers?" Jake stabbed his own pancakes and slathered them with butter and syrup.

"I do believe he hears and answers my prayers in a way that's best for me. They don't always turn out the way I want them answered, though. But I still trust him."

"Well, he never answered my prayers to keep my mom and dad together," Jake admitted before changing topics. "I think I'll still be on guard for you. I'll see you at lunch and then pick you up after work."

"I appreciate all you're doing. If you don't mind bringing pizza for lunch, we can eat at the park with the dogs. I think your help is part of the answer to my prayer." She smiled and pushed back from the table, preparing to go and get ready for work.

"Well … ?" Jake let out the word as a question.

"What?"

"I can't believe my cooking made such an impression." Jake pouted.

"You, Jake, are a great cook." She stood on tiptoe and kissed his cheek.

"Is my cooking a way to your heart?"

"I'm not sure yet." She patted his chest. "Let's see what happens when you cook dinner." She twirled and ran up to get ready for work.

She heard the clinking of dishes while she dressed for work and couldn't believe how thoughtful he was … but he *could* be a little overprotective. She trod down the stairs and met Jake and the dogs in the hallway.

"I'll be following you to work and then I'll bring pizza for lunch." Jake wrapped her in a hug and gently warmed her lips with his.

"Thanks for everything." Miranda reached for Doc's leash. "I have you, Doc, and the patrolling deputies. See you at lunch."

"I almost forgot to ask if you have any new clients today?"

150

She understood the underlying worry behind that question. Was there a possibility that the writer of the note might pose as a client? "All today's clients are ones I have seen previously." She patted his arm reassuringly. "If I see anything unusual I'll call you and Nick right away."

As Miranda pulled out, she glanced in her rearview mirror and saw Jake pull out behind and follow her. As she turned onto Main Street, uneasiness crept into her mind. *Was the note in the mailbox just to scare me or was it a real threat on my life? Lord, please calm my anxious thoughts.*

A honk behind her startled her. She looked up and saw a man's wide eyes and open mouth as he froze in the crosswalk just in front of her. She slammed on the brakes, tires squealing, stopping just in time. Her head slumped to the steering wheel, and she took a quieting deep breath before opening her window to apologize. Her near-victim thumped the hood of her car and yelled, "Watch out, lady." In the rearview mirror, she saw Jake mouth, *Be careful.* With one more fortifying breath she proceeded to work. What a way to start the workday.

Once in the office, she began working which calmed her mind enough to be attentive to her clients. As promised, Jake brought pizza, and they shared it at the park, letting the dogs chase a Frisbee and each other. Jake walked her back to the office and reminded her that he'd be back at 5:30.

"Please Miranda, wait until I come up to get you."

"I'll be careful." It was the only thing she could promise. Something urgent might come up so she couldn't promise to wait. "I'll call if there is some emergency," she conceded.

The afternoon passed uneventfully, and Rachel took off early to get her daughter to the dentist.

"Have a great weekend and give each of your daughters a hug for me," Miranda called out to Rachel.

"Thanks. You too."

The office was quiet. As she expected no more clients that day, Miranda let Doc out of his crate, locked the office door, and then sat at her desk pulling the files for the next week's appointments. Her phone alarm interrupted her studying. It was time for Jake to pick her up and he hadn't called to announce his arrival. Something must have delayed him. She pushed the speed dial for his cell, but it went straight to voicemail. She tried again with the same result.

The tingling started in her limbs and moved to her torso; she started pacing. Jake still hadn't called or arrived. She needed to go—now. Something could be wrong. She felt deep down that she needed to go and was thankful she'd driven her own car.

Fumbling with the leash clip, she finally was able to attach it to Doc's collar. In a whirlwind, she locked the door, flew down the stairs, and pulled by Doc, flew out of the building.

All the leaves had been raked and deposited into the bins he carried with him. The garden beds had been cleaned up for Mr. Green. Jake twisted his wrist to check his watch and saw it was almost 4:30. He had to leave right away to make it back to Stone Ridge so he could make sure Miranda was okay. As he'd worked that day, Jake's thoughts had been focused on Miranda's trust in God and that he answers her prayers. She hadn't expected they would all be answered the way she wanted, but that he'd answer in the way that was best for her.

Had God's ignoring his request for his family to get back together been the best thing for him and his mom? Maybe, because one thing Jake knew for sure was that he couldn't forgive his father like his mom had done years earlier. The man hadn't even tried to get in touch with Jake until he was well into his teen years, so Jake was returning the favor, much to his mother's dismay. He didn't know how God could expect him to forgive a dad who didn't even pay child support on time. His mom had tried to hide that fact, but Jake knew how she'd struggled until her business had finally taken off. Best to get his mind off that subject.

Before he could leave, he had a few little things to clean-up, and he needed to finish his signature edging and cleaning the moss off the pavers.

When he'd arrived he'd checked to see if the payment was under the mat, half hoping it wasn't there so he could leave. Doing this job could lead to growing his business; he hoped eventually to use his degree in architectural landscaping, too. To his surprise, the envelope was there and instead of the usual half, Mr. Green had left the full payment with a tip. Jake hoped this client turned out to be a good referral!

His phone vibrated and looking at the caller ID he saw a familiar number. "Hello?"

"Hello, Jake. Are you almost finished?" After a brief hesitation, the man identified himself. "This is Rodney Green checking in."

"Oh, yes I'm just about to pack up and leave. Thanks for the full payment and tip. You didn't have to do that." Jake held the phone tightly.

"Well, you are a fast worker. I expected it would take another hour or so longer than your quote. Could you do me a favor? I have some dead plants in the greenhouse. Would you round them up and dispose of them? I'd appreciate it. Please take the pots they're in, too."

"Sure. I think I can finish that before I have to leave." Jake began moving in the direction of the greenhouse.

"Thanks." And without saying goodbye, he hung up.

Jake slowly made his way toward the greenhouse, perusing the yard for anything he may have missed. He peered into the burn barrel and pulled out a couple of petals that looked burned and held on to them as he entered the greenhouse.

The place was a mess; it was filled with pots with dead plants and a workbench that hadn't been used in years. There *was* one small area that seemed to have been used more recently.

Jake heard a click behind him, and as he did, he twirled to see a shadow slither into the hedges through the greenhouse walls. He strode to the door and tried to turn the knob. It was locked. Who put a lock on a greenhouse? One to keep someone inside, not prowlers out? He shook the door; it was solid and the lock secure. He stood hands fisted deciding what he should do.

Jake took in a deep breath and unfurled his hands, and the petals dropped to the dirt floor. He bent to pick them up, at that instant he knew what they were—they hadn't simply been burned, they were black rose petals.

He pulled out his cellphone, but he couldn't get a signal inside the greenhouse. He had to get out to call Nick! He knew who was after Miranda.

He'd parked his nondescript car across from Miranda's office building and was slumped behind the wheel waiting for her to exit. He'd practiced the U-turn needed to put the car in place. He'd checked the backseat for all the tools he'd need: rope, tape, gun, and tire iron. He'd also set up the bait for the dog.

Now he sat and observed, waiting for his chance. Would she come out alone or would she wait for Jake? He knew Jake wouldn't show up soon. He'd received the call and was told Jake was safely locked in the greenhouse. If investigated, the professor couldn't be blamed for that. After all, he'd finished his classes for the day and wasn't going to show up at home until much later.

Police officers were patrolling the area each hour on the hour, and the last one had been by a half an hour earlier. He had planned everything to the minute. It would only take five minutes to get her into the car. Then the fun would begin.

He caught a movement and shadow coming toward him on the left. He lifted the newspaper to hide his face, something he hadn't thought to do earlier when Miranda was around. *She may not know I am the one, but she is close to figuring it out, so her fate is sealed.*

CHAPTER TWENTY

FRIDAY, OCTOBER 25TH

NIGHTTIME

Patience had paid off. The professor had been sitting in his car across the street from Miranda's office building for three hours. He watched as she surged out the doors wagging her head from side-to-side frantically. Then, he saw the dog catch the scent of the *treat* he'd left—perfect! He opened his window a tad to listen. Miranda said, "Leave it," but the dog had already half swallowed the tainted meat.

Holding his breath, he counted to twenty-five, then, as if on cue, the dog staggered and sank to the ground. He swiveled his head to see if anyone was coming. No. Good, it was clear, and there were still another twenty minutes before an officer would walk down the street. He executed his U-turn perfectly and smoothly. Miranda hadn't even glanced in his direction.

He was about to get out of his car, but someone exited the bookstore across the street. He looked as though he was going to cross the street to help Miranda with her dog. The professor quickly climbed out of his car and waved to get the man's attention and motioned he would help. *Get out of here, mister, and quickly.* He let out a slow breath as the man nodded and walked away. A phrase from a song came to mind:

"Everything's going my way." And it couldn't be more perfect. This was meant to be.

Miranda heaved open the office doors and desperately wished to see a red Dodge coming from either direction, but to no avail. Doc jerked her to the left and half dragged her forward. She stumbled and then caught her balance, but not before she saw Doc's jaws open to grab something. He was always finding something to put in his mouth. They'd been practicing the *leave it* command, but before she could even get the word out, he'd swallowed whatever it was.

Doc started staggering and in less than thirty seconds was down and breathing fast, looking up at her with soulful eyes as if to ask, *What is happening and please make it go away.* "Doc, what have you eaten?" she moaned softly in his ear and then reached for her phone. She couldn't carry the dog quickly enough to get help, and the veterinary clinic was on speed dial.

Tremors started deep within and slowly moved up her torso and through her arms, across her shoulders, then eventually creeping up her neck and on toward her face. She fumbled with the phone, shaking and with fingers twitching, she finally managed to punch the right number. With her other hand, she tried to get Doc to stand, but he couldn't move.

Tears streamed down her cheeks, dripping like rain onto her dog. The vet office answered. "Hello."

"Please come. My dog he has eaten something bad."

"Ma'am who are you?"

"Miranda." She barely got the name out before she was jolted up by strong hands which grasped her arms, pinning them to her side. Her cell went flying out of her hand crashing to the sidewalk. She opened her mouth to scream, but a towel was stuffed into it, and a hand covered her mouth and nose so she couldn't breathe. He held her, facing her toward her dog, allowing her to see Doc's muscles twitching and his eyes still pleading for her help. Then, he swiftly twisted her away. He'd had to let go of one of her arms to cover her face, and she grabbed his little finger and pulled hard. He mumbled something unintelligible as his hand loosened. She had just enough time to take in a short breath before he strengthened his grip. He jerked the arm he already held behind her back and shoving her to the car.

She remembered this car. It had been parked around here a couple of times and … it looked like the same car that had run her off the road Wednesday evening! *Who is this monster? Worse—how would anyone find her now?*

Miranda's head hit the side of the car as he shoved her inside, momentarily stunning her, which gave him enough time to get her on the seat and clip the seatbelt tight, nearly strangling her with pressure. She still couldn't breathe, and blackness was closing in. Somehow, even without being able to breathe, an overpowering aroma of roses filled her senses, and she felt nauseated.

Oh Lord, my dog. And Jake, where is he? She longed for his scent of pine cologne and hard work, for his comforting arms holding her and protecting her from this nightmare.

She tried to hold on to consciousness, to frantically look around for help. Just before completely losing the battle she saw the red truck. *Lord, please let him see me and rescue me!*

She'd give one last try to stop this maniac and get him to let go. She kicked him with all the strength she had left and felt the connection with soft flesh as pain shot through her foot. Numbness covered her body as hopelessness enveloped her mind. Oh, my poor Doc.

"Ouch, you little …" She didn't hear another word.

The professor raced to the other side of the car after first making sure no one was in sight. He hopped in and pulled out a pillow to prop Miranda's head on so she looked as though she was napping. He jammed the key in the ignition and slowly pulled away from the curb and away from the office building.

He watched in his rearview mirror to make sure he hadn't been followed and what he saw stunned his senses. Jake was in front of Miranda's office building, standing and holding something, staring in his direction! His truck was parked in the same spot the professor had just vacated. *I can't panic. How did Jake get out of my greenhouse and make it here?* He slammed on the brakes at the stop sign. *Steady. Watch what you're doing.* He took another quick peek back and then relaxed. The truck was still parked, and Jake had disappeared. Thankful once more that he'd rented this common vehicle—and under an alias—he knew he would be okay.

It was time to park behind the convenience store and prepare Miranda for the rest of the trip. Quickly, he pulled out the rope and tape. He taped her mouth then tied her ankles. They were nice and slender, but he had better not think like that and get his mind back on the work at hand. He tied her hands behind her back, and as he was positioning her again, a young man walked toward them. With a hand on either side of her face, the professor bent as if to kiss limp lips, but he continued to watch as the stranger reversed direction.

He straightened behind the wheel and weaved his way through a neighborhood before easing into the traffic onto the road which led to his privately-owned cabin near the state park. After checking to make sure there wasn't anyone following, he relaxed and let the same phrase, *Everything's going my way,* repeat like a broken record in his mind. Miranda's head bobbed a bit, but it was mostly set on the pillow, still.

There was still another half-hour before reaching his destination, so his thoughts took a more pleasant track. Miranda was a pretty little thing; too bad she'd unintentionally crossed his path at the wrong time. She knew Valerie. If he allowed much more time to go by, the two ladies might get close to putting it all together. Then his business and livelihood would be gone. After he took care of Miranda, he had to make sure Valerie couldn't talk anymore either.

Jake slammed on the brakes. The tires screeched as the truck slid to a stop, occupying the space a white sedan had just vacated. He saw an object on the sidewalk and picked it up. Someone's iPhone. He stared at the retreating sedan and got as much of a plate number as possible, thinking he would give it to the police if they needed it for some reason.

Miranda! He crashed through the swinging doors and flew up the stairs, grabbing and pulling on the locked door. He pounded his fist on the door and waited impatiently. No dog bark and no movement from inside. He willed her come and open the door. He fought with the knob once more. He dialed her number on his cell and heard ringing and vibrating in his other hand. *Oh no! Lord, please no!* He was holding *Miranda's* cellphone!

He hung up and dialed Nick as he raced down and back outside. Scanning the area to see if he could catch a glimpse of the car again he noticed a dark lump. "Doc!" Jake wailed as he approached the dog. His EMT training kicked in and he felt for a heartbeat. There was a very weak pulse—but it was there—so he scooped up the pup and deposited him in the front seat of his truck, covering the pup with a blanket from the back of the truck. He raced around and started driving frantically with no thought of speed limits to the veterinary clinic and dialed 911 at the same time.

"This is 911. What is your emergency?"

Jake explained the best he could about the dog and that he believed Miranda had been kidnapped and that he knew who had done it.

"I'll have an officer meet you at the veterinary office. And we will locate Nick."

Jake heard the intermittent sound of a police siren. He looked in the rearview mirror to see it was him they were pulling over. *Could anything else go wrong, Lord?* He was speaking to God. *How odd.*

Miranda's head throbbed as it was jostled against something soft, and her thoughts were disoriented. She struggled to remember something, anything: stooping by her dog, her head banging something hard, and her foot aching. She tried opening her eyes, but a stabbing pain caused her to clamp them shut once more. She was nauseated. Little bits of the puzzle came to her, but not enough pieces to put it together and why was she swaying? She listened and heard the hum of a car engine. *Whose car and where is it going? Lord, help!*

The car lurched to the right, and her head throbbed even more as the car bumped along over random ruts. She wanted to vomit but swallowed hard and again tried to pry her eyes open. It was darker here, and she took in the wilderness—a familiar sight from her hikes with Jake earlier in the week. She was going to find out where she was and who this person was, but she couldn't open her mouth or move her hands from behind her back. She glanced from the corner of her eyes to glimpse the driver and gasped. *Him! That professor at the grocery store and the college. Lord, get me away from him!*

"Ah, I see you are finally awake, and I can see recognition in your face. This was the first time I tried the technique of waiting for you to lose consciousness with no oxygen. It worked nicely instead of having to find chloroform once more. I read about it on the Internet. Oh. Don't worry about your dog. Another Internet search found a quick-acting drug. He didn't feel any pain." At his callous words, tears slid in rivulets down her cheeks.

Everything in her wanted to kick the man and get out of the car, but she was tied up, and her feet and hands were numb. She needed to get the feeling back in them if she stood a chance of doing anything to help herself. She wiggled her hands and feet and finally felt the life come back in stinging rhythm. She tried in vain to loosen her bindings.

The trees and brush closed in on them, and there was scraping against the car. It grated on her nerves like fingernails screeching down a blackboard. *Let it go. Think. There has to be a way to escape.* A calm enveloped her, and she knew it was God's peace because she wasn't shaking anymore. She needed to keep this man talking and bragging, but her mouth was taped shut.

"You're awfully quiet. Ha-ha-ha." A sinister cackle filled the air along with the overpowering scent of roses. "Things really do seem to be going my way. Jake and your dog are safely out of the way for the first time. Somehow, you were able to get away from me twice. Once in the parking lot when you left the truck. Ah, I see you remember and yes, that was me. The second time was when your dog helped drag you into the ditch. Why did you leave the truck?" He was silent for a few seconds. "Oh, my. You—can't—talk."

This evil person did something to Jake, but I saw his truck. Lord, please help him to put the pieces together and maybe save Doc, too.

"My plan was always to bring you here, so you see, I had a backup all along. When we reach my cabin, which by the way is well-hidden, the games begin. I do suppose you are wondering how I found out who you are. Well, the little clerk was carrying your card. I thought I'd find out whose card she was carrying and what luck! It was you."

Maybe the police could identify this professor by going back to the grocery store. Miranda felt guilty she hadn't been able to stop the man from killing the clerk. She realized it wasn't her fault, but guilt came so easily after what had happened with her sister. Then, it dawned on her that the professor hadn't mentioned anything about her sister. Her sister didn't seem to be in his sights at all. *Lord, keep Jenny safe.*

"Did you enjoy all the roses that greeted you at home, at the office, and in your mailbox? That note was prophetic, and here we are. I destroyed any evidence linking me to black roses," he sneered. "After tonight, I'll go back to finish off Valerie."

Miranda couldn't have a defeated outlook. She needed to believe God would somehow intervene, and this evil human could be stopped.

"By the way, how did you find Valerie? Oops, that's right you can't talk. Just as well. I like hearing myself talk uninterrupted." His voice quieted simultaneously with the car shuddering to a stop.

Miranda's hopes dropped out from under her. She saw the front of the cabin and it reminded her of the soddies she'd seen in historical sites, except that this cabin was covered not only with moss with trees growing out of it, but with brambles, and had spindly vines hanging over the front. The only open space was now filled with the car. Where could she even run to if she could get free?

"Here we are, at the hidden Green Cabin. How do you like it?" He exited the car and circled to open the door before yanking her out. Miranda tumbled, but with a determined effort, dug her heels into the soft ground as the professor tried to drag her to the cabin. She heard him swear under his breath and was surprised he didn't hoist her over his shoulder. She tensed when he pulled out a knife. *Lord, is this already the end?*

No! He had bent down and sliced the rope that clamped her ankles. With the strength given by adrenaline she jerked her knee into his face and felt the crunch of his nose and then the warm stickiness as the blood spurted out.

His scream pierced the dusk.

She felt lightheaded and wobbly, but adrenaline kicked in once more as she saw her chance to escape. Twisting, she darted into the unknown wilderness, going as fast as her high heels and hands tied behind her back would allow.

CHAPTER TWENTY-ONE

FRIDAY, OCTOBER 25

6:00 PM

Jake slowed the truck. The patrol car was still on his tail, and he looked to see who was driving it and winced. It was Pete Sweete. The guy had it in for him. Jake didn't know what he had done to get on the man's bad side, except have long hair. He'd give a quick explanation and leave.

"Well, well, well. I knew you would show your true colors sooner or later. You were doing fifty miles per hour in a twenty-five miles per hour zone …"

"I know. I have a dog that needs immediate attention, or he will die. Call the 911 dispatcher, but I have to go. I'll be at the vet's office," Jake yelled out the window as he punched the gas and left the officer in his dust. He hoped the other officers would back him up and explain the situation. If not, Pete would get what he'd been hoping for ever since Jake had moved to town.

Once he reached the vet office, Jake stopped as carefully as he could, jumped out of the truck, and sprinted to the other side. He carefully tucked Doc against him and carried the dog into the office.

"Hi, Jake." Lacie's eyes brightened with surprise, and he knew her smile meant more than just a simple greeting.

"Hi. This is Doc, Miranda's dog, and I don't know what's wrong, but he has a weak pulse."

Lacie called out instructions. The immediate action taken by her employees told Jake that she was a great veterinarian. They took the dog from him and then went in the back. Jake knew Lacie liked him, but he hadn't done anything to encourage a relationship other than a professional one as regarded the dogs. He'd eaten dinner with her once because there was only one table available at the café, and she hadn't wanted to eat alone. She was nice—but Miranda had captured his heart. *Miranda! Lord, rescue her.*

He punched in Nick's number once more, and it rolled to voicemail again. The operator said she would contact Nick, so hopefully Nick was apprised of the situation.

The door swung open, and Pete swaggered into the vet's office. *What else will go wrong?*

"I can have you put in jail for taking off," Pete drawled.

"I know. Are you going to do it?" Jake asked drawing his hand across his face.

"Not this time, but you will get a speeding ticket for going twenty-five miles per hour over the speed limit."

Jake's phone rang. Ignoring the deputy, he answered. "Nick, where are you?"

"At the hospital. What's going on Jake? The dispatcher said it was an emergency."

"It is." Jake relayed all that had happened while Pete dangled the ticket in front of Jake's face. He snatched it and asked Nick to hold for a second. "Do you have my cell number?" he asked the receptionist.

"Yes," she answered and rattled it off just to make sure.

"Thanks, call me with any updates." Jake saw her nod, and he whooshed past Pete and into his truck. Still on the phone, he asked Nick, "Where can I meet you?"

"Let's meet at the station."

It didn't take long to drive there, and once there, Jake headed directly for Nick's desk. "Well, what are we going to do? I know this is the guy who took Miranda. We need to find her before he has a chance to hurt her."

"Jake, calm down. Tell me from the beginning what happened."

Jake told the detective how he got a last minute job.

"Why did you take the job? It's quite a distance from here."

"Because it's a neighborhood where I've been trying to solicit business and hopefully to get back into doing some architectural landscaping. Nick, what difference could that possibly make? We have to find Miranda. Look, when I was there, I picked up these." He drew two black rose petals from his pocket and handed them to Nick. "He is the one sending those flowers and I was locked into the greenhouse by someone I didn't see. I had to break down the door to get out and get back to pick up Miranda. But by the time I got back, she was gone, and Doc was almost dead. I saw a car pull away. It was a white Honda Civic and I got the partial plate." He told Nick the letter and numbers and watched the detective write it down.

After he had finished, Nick spoke. "I was at the hospital because Valerie was coming out of consciousness for short periods of time. She kept mentioning night flowers. And we've been to the grocery store where both women worked. They did see a man visit with Valerie several times—he is the professor at the college. The college said the professor told them he was going to visit his family this weekend and took today off."

"That can't be right. He told me he was going to have a big gathering at his house and that's why I needed to do the job as quickly as possible. He has to be the one."

Nick showed a picture to Jake. "Is this the man you talked with on Thursday?"

Jake shook his head. "If this is Rodney Green, then who did I see?"

"I don't know. Are you sure Miranda was supposed to meet you? Is her car still there?" Nick asked.

"I took off so quickly I didn't even think to look for her car," Jake admitted.

"I'll call the officer patrolling the area. What kind of car does she drive?"

Jake answered Nick, and he even had the license plate number.

While they waited, Jake remembered Miranda's cell in his pocket.

"I have her cell phone." He handed it to Nick. Nick punched some keys and looked up.

"She called the vet office just before you got to her. I'll get the guys working on that partial plate. Jake, I think you need to call in the SAR team." Nick called his team with the plate numbers.

"Where should they meet up and start looking?" Jake asked as he tugged his phone out.

"Let's start where it all began. I'll call the college to get any more information on this professor."

"Thanks, Nick. I'll call them on my way home so I can meet them." Jake waved and pushed out the station doors.

Jake sped through his condo in a whirlwind, changing and letting Katie out of her crate, grabbing the leash and his already packed backpack. Katie pranced alongside Jake on the way to the truck and then jumped in as the door opened. Jake sped to the state park. *Lord, help us to find Miranda quickly. Keep her safe.* There he went again, praying. He only hoped God would listen to him this time. But if he chose to believe like Miranda did, then God had listened to him when his dad took off too. Why did God let those things happen? Jake was still stuck in the bitterness of not forgiving his father, but could he forgive God for not answering the way he had wanted him to answer? According to Miranda, God answers for our best, but his dad did what he wanted for himself with no thought for Jake or Jake's mother. Maybe God let his father leave and maybe it was for the best since the fights had stopped, and his mother actually had been happy. Jake still couldn't forgive his father. The man didn't deserve forgiveness.

Oh, God, please don't let anything happen to Miranda. She is kind, thoughtful, compassionate, and wise and she is holding more and more of my heart. I need to find her.

CHAPTER TWENTY-TWO

FRIDAY, OCTOBER 25

6:30 PM

Tripping over roots, stumbling and pushing through brush with her hands tied behind her and wearing two-inch heels was like trying to swim upstream in a river, fully clothed. Miranda kept staggering forward, making slow progress as brambles attached to her coat like leeches. They caught on her hair, left scratches on her face and put runs in her nylons, leaving welt lines on her flesh as they did. But she kept forging ahead though terrified of what might happen as she went deeper into the woods. Beams of light still shone through the tangles of trees; she wildly swung her head from side to side, trying to find the best place to hide. Miranda tried to stay balanced on her toes so the heels wouldn't sink, but then the heel caught on a root that sent her tumbling down. She watched in slow motion; a rock was about to meet her face, but she twisted away at the last moment, landing hard which caused a sharp pain to shoot through her shoulder.

She let her head droop to the ground. Tears stung behind her eyes, waiting for her to give up so they could fall. *No, I won't give up.* She listened for anything that sounded like someone following her. The only things she heard were birds and squirrels telling her off. Miranda rocked her body into a sitting position and with her good arm pushed up to her feet once more. Dizziness hit for an instant, and she took in a deep breath then continued to seek a place to hide.

Off to the left, she saw a small tunnel-like hole in a thicket that looked like a patch of dead branches. She dropped to her knees and lowered her head to shove herself into the small space. Needle pricks from the thorns impaled her through her coat and skirt, but her need to survive forced her to ignore them as much as possible.

I am your strength. His voice talked to her, and she remembered what he had gone through for her, so she continued to forge ahead into a small but hollow alcove. It was impassable from there. She tried to maneuver into a more comfortable position but struck something hard and sharp. She let out a yelp.

Covering her mouth, she listened. It was getting darker, and the owls hooted, and the coyotes started howling. The birds had quieted. She didn't hear any rustling or branches breaking—she was okay. But how far behind was this madman? He knew these woods, and he was dressed for the wilderness. Miranda shuddered and tried to think of what to do next.

Cautiously, she reached behind her to explore, feeling the sharp, jagged edge of what seemed to be a rock. Had she subconsciously been praying for a way to get the rope off? Was this God's answer? She'd thank the Almighty for this gift. She started a sawing motion with the rope against the rough edge of the rock and finally felt a little snap. A strand must have broken!

She stopped and listened. The light was fading fast, and she was draped in quiet darkness. She sniffed. If he was nearby, the overpowering odor of roses would follow him, but she only inhaled cool night air filled with the scents of pine and damp moss. She went back to working the rope back and forth, up and down, against the ragged edge. Another strand broke and then another, but the rope still held fast. She needed to hurry! Just as another strand broke, she heard the crack of a branch.

Miranda froze. She heard another sound of brushing against tree branches, and then it went quiet once more. She let out her breath slowly and went back to work on the rope. Finally, it snapped off her wrist. She brought her arms in front of her, wincing at the pain in her left shoulder. Keeping the shoulder still, she rubbed her wrists and arms, warming them, and at the same time getting the circulation moving again. She then carefully peeled the tape from her mouth and spat out the rag. It took a few minutes to get the saliva flowing again to relieve her dry mouth and scratchy throat.

What was her next move? Should she stay where she was and take her chances of being well hidden, or should she move to a new location? She might want to move to a new location. She hadn't gone far before finding this hole. She thought she was still fairly close to the cabin.

A scream that sliced the quiet told her he wasn't far behind.

"Miranda, I will get you. You won't even know until I strike." It sounded staccato—each word enunciated as he fought to give her a death message.

Move on, an inner voice urged, but Miranda couldn't move.

So she thought she could get away from me. His nose was painful, and blood kept spurting, but he didn't think it was broken. He'd given her a little time to try and hide from him, leisurely going into the cabin and taking a couple of aspirin for the pain, swallowing four of them without water. The bitter taste fueled his anger against Miranda. She'd tried this twice before, but, this time, was different because *he* had the advantage. He'd grown up in these woods. Dark or not, he would find her.

How far could she have gone with her wrists tied behind her back and while wearing high heels? No contest—he was already the winner. His father had taught him how to be a cunning hunter, how to be as quiet as a cat. They'd always come home with some game, usually illegal, he'd learned later. He questioned his father about it once, and his father tersely answered. "It's our land, and no law can keep us from putting food on our table. You will keep your mouth shut, and no one will know about it."

The professor, Rodney, had been a young boy at the time and didn't keep his mouth shut. Instead, he bragged to a friend. Rodney's father had found out about it and took his son to the cabin, expressing his displeasure in a physical way. Rodney learned to hide everything that day. That was why his drug business was so successful; the cops hadn't been able to break it up. To keep it that way, he'd had to take care of some loose-tongued women and one stepbrother.

He went to his car and drew out the knife, checked the blade, and then slid it into its sheath. He then stuffed a gun under his belt and grabbed the tire iron, along with a flashlight. He was ready for the hunt.

Miranda's trail was easy to follow, and he thought he knew where she was hiding. He clicked off his light and took one step to the right and then another, but intense, stabbing pains climbed his leg. He hopped back and to the left on the good leg, but lost his balance and fell into the brambles. Something clamped so hard on his arm he was sure it was broken. It could only have been a trap he'd set years ago. He stared at a porcupine waddling away from him and cursed.

He cursed again, yelling threats through excruciating pain, and blaming Miranda. Rage engulfed him, and his only thought was of revenge.

Miranda sensed another nudge to move on, but she felt safe where she was and after the screaming, she hadn't heard another sound. Brambles covered her, and she couldn't get far with heels. She needed a weapon.

She tried to dig out the jagged-edged rock she'd used to cut her ropes, but it wouldn't budge.

Move on! Don't stay! The urging grew more insistent. If she was going to move, she had to get rid of the heels. But she needed shoes. All right then, the rock would have more than one use. She pulled off her shoes and whacked the two-inch heels against the sharp rock, and slipped them back on as flats. She ripped strips from her coat to tie around her knees for a little protection against the stickers. After securing her left arm tightly against her chest with her belt, she moved awkwardly toward the opening, listening every few seconds, trying to hear anything unusual.

Finally, once back on the trail, she looked behind to see if there was anyone or any light around her. It was mostly black and silent. She tottered in the broken shoes, trying to remember some of the survival techniques Jake had taught her on their recent hikes. Had it only been three days earlier that she'd been on that last hike with Jake? The temperature dropped, and her lightweight coat wasn't going to be much help. She needed shelter—but off the trail. Could she cover her tracks enough to hide her presence?

Exhausted from this trek and anxious, she easily lost her footing and tripped hard; unable to catch her balance, she tumbled forward. Miranda clenched her teeth, ignoring the agony in her shoulder, willing her body to stand up again and move on. Then she jumped as an owl screeched. What other wildlife might she encounter?

What were the chances of this city girl surviving a night of a maniac trying to kill her and with wildlife stalking her? She couldn't remember what Jake had taught her. *Oh Lord, if ever I needed help, it would be now.* And then … peace entered her inner being.

Off to the right she spotted a little opening which might have been easily missed, but with God's eyes, it was seen. She went a distance about the length of a football field past the trail and then backtracked to the almost-hidden path. She picked up a few evergreen branches, blown to the ground by the wind, and backed into the path, brushing out her footprints.

She pushed through branches and ferns, shuddering at every little noise. If he were around, he would certainly hit her from behind without her realizing he was there. The eerie quiet punctuated by little squeals, crackles, and hoots reminded Miranda of a climactic scene in old horror films—but this was real, not on the screen. She took a deep breath to calm her uneasy thoughts. She was afraid, but not in a panicked state. God must be with her ... if only he might tell her what to do next.

CHAPTER TWENTY-THREE

SATURDAY, OCTOBER 26TH

4:00 AM

The radio crackled with yet another disappointing message. They'd been sending out teams since 8:00 the night before, but in eight hours they'd found no sign of Miranda or the professor. Anne was coming in to rest her dog for the second time.

"No indication anyone has been here. My dog is tired; I'd like to take a break."

"That's fine, come on back. We have a fresh team to send out."

Jake had been at the base camp the whole eight hours. The only thing keeping him awake was the enormous amount of caffeine he'd ingested. He bowed his head. *Lord, please help us find her.*

"Were you praying?" Anne surprised him by coming from behind.

"Yeah, but it doesn't seem to do any good. Where is she?" He shook his head.

"Prayer is always heard." Anne gently touched his arm.

"That's what Miranda says too. So I found I was talking with God a lot recently. How are you holding up?" He stooped to pet her dog.

"We're doing well. I think we need an hour's nap before going out again. And Jake—don't stop praying. God hears. Will we see you at church, too?" She headed to her SUV, her dog following.

"Maybe," he answered.

A vibration in his pocket startled Jake. He ripped the phone out and swiped to answer the call. "Nick, any news on Miranda?"

"No, but I have other information that may help us find her. Keep the search going, but make sure they know we may move to another area at a moment's notice."

"Okay, I'll pass on the information." Jake clicked off the call and ran to the head of operations. "Nick just called and wants you to keep up the search. I'm going to meet him because he has another lead and may need you to move quickly."

"Fine, we'll keep in touch."

Jake grabbed his pack from his back and stuffed his flashlight in the side pocket. Then, with the light from the sun slowly rising above the peaks, he jogged to the park entrance.

Please God, let this be the clue we've been looking for to find Miranda. If she's okay, I promise I'll go to church. Not a maybe anymore. Prove you are real.

"Jake," Nick called out.

"What did you find out?" Jake rushed up to Nick's car.

"We know the professor owns a cabin on the other side of the state park. Get in and we'll go there." Nick unlocked the doors.

"I have to get Katie. I can't leave my dog in the truck as the sun comes up. She could bake in there. I can follow you if you like," Jake offered.

"No, go ahead and bring her, but make sure she has something to chew on besides the car's upholstery." He lifted one eyebrow.

Jake jogged to the car and let Katie out. She went over to the weeded area to do her business then happily jumped in the detective's car, carrying the chew toy Jake gave her. Jake slid in the passenger side.

"How did you find out about the cabin?"

"We did an Internet search and found out a lot about him. He was an only child, and his mother died when he was in his teens. His father remarried, and after he died the professor didn't have any contact with the stepmother. We called her, and she thought there was a cabin her husband mentioned. Well, during another search we found it. That's where we're headed."

"How far away is it?"

"It's quite a way out yet. If that's where they are, it stands to reason the dogs haven't found anything yet. Have you heard from the vet about Miranda's dog?" Nick remembered all the details. No wonder he was a good detective.

"Let me check." Jake swiped the screen and saw he had a new text. It was from the veterinary clinic. "Yes, this text says he is stable, and it looks like he will recover. Now, we just need to find Miranda and tell her."

"We're close now. The cabin is at the end of this dirt road."

Jake noticed trees and brush closing in on them as the road narrowed to two tracks. Nick's car bounced and rocked until they finally stopped behind a patrol car.

Both men shoved their doors open and met the officer.

"What did you guys find?" Nick asked.

"You'd better come here, sir."

Nick motioned to Jake to remain in the car, and with his coat flapping, he followed the officer.

Jake understood the protocol and stayed nearby the car, but everything in him wanted to go too. He might see something they'd miss. He peeked in the car, seeing Katie happily chew on her treat-filled toy. He started channeling a groove around the cars as he paced and watched the men stoop to look at something before they entered a cabin overgrown with brambles and moss. *Lord, Miranda has to be alive.* Jake clung to that hope.

Nick appeared in the doorway and walked toward Jake. His face didn't give anything away.

"Well?" The question hung in the air.

"We're pretty sure both Miranda and the professor were here. There is one set of prints going toward and entering the cabin. Looks to be a man-size shoe, so probably the professor's. We also saw a smaller shoe print with heels going into the woods opposite the cabin. Probably

Miranda's. Where both prints are together, there is blood on the ground and a cut rope."

"Whose blood?" Jake stiffened.

"We're pretty sure it's the professor's because there is also blood in the cabin and he seems to be the only one who entered the cabin," Nick explained. Jake let out a breath.

"What's next?"

"I'm going to call in a K-9 unit and call off the SAR search. In the meantime, the officers and I will follow the trail, tracking the professor."

"I'm going, too." Jake lifted his chin and looked Nick square in the eyes daring him to refuse.

Nick shook his head.

"I'm an EMT. You may need me. Miranda may need me. Even the professor may need me." Jake left to get his pack and put Katie on a leash.

"You stay in the back, then. The man is unpredictable, and he may have a gun," Nick warned.

Jake's thoughts turned to Miranda. *Where was she? Had the professor found her? Was she still alive?* Deep inside he felt she was still alive. *Please keep her safe, God.* There, he'd done it again. Praying had become a habit when there wasn't anything else he could do. Remarkably, his nerves quieted, and Jake was able to follow silently.

The men stopped. All of them saw some cloth clutched in an old trap and more blood.

"Does this look familiar to you?" Nick drew Jake closer.

"No, I've never seen anything like it before," Jake answered.

"Good, then it's probably the professor's. Caught in his own trap. Look at the porcupine needles lying about. It looks as though he got it good. We may need you yet, Jake."

Jake didn't want anything to do with the man who'd threatened Miranda. As far as he was concerned, the professor could wait for the paramedics. Jake's skills might be needed for Miranda.

Now it was daylight, and every little thing was visible. The men stopped again. On the ground were heel shoe prints which pointed to a small opening. Next, Jake saw two sets of prints headed down the trail. This time, there were no heel holes in the ground.

"She must have shed the heels. Smart girl," Nick commented.

They needed to find Miranda soon. Jake would never forgive himself for getting her into this mess. If he hadn't asked her to go on SAR training, she would never have known about Valerie, or the professor, or the clerk. If she were still alive, she was probably in agony.

" … only see a man-size shoe from here."

Jakes self-guilt thinking was interrupted.

"Let's continue to see if the professor is ahead, or if he's trying to throw us off." Nick led the way.

Progress was unbearably slow, but Jake knew how detailed they had to be and check out any clues while examining the trail. They regularly stopped to look behind themselves, too, just in case they could spot something from a different angle. Katie started pulling on the leash to go back the way they'd come, and Jake tugged her back. She then ran for it, and when she hit the end of the leash, her front feet raised above the ground. Finally, Jake had to give her a couple of leash corrections. She settled, but continued to look behind them and whine.

Jake's head snapped up from looking at the ground as Nick yelled, "Hands up. Did you hear me? Police! Put your hands up."

Jake looked past the officers and noticed a man slumped on the ground, holding his arm, rocking and moaning. He'd let the police check out this guy; he could be faking it.

The officers raised their guns and slowly crept up to the rocking figure.

"Are you Professor Rodney Green?" Nick asked.

The man tilted his head up, and Jake saw the pain in his eyes. Besides the bleeding arm, the man's eyes were turning black and blue. Jake looked at Nick to question whether or not to help the guy. Nick shook his head.

"How far away is the K-9 unit?" Nick called someone on his cell.

"Okay, and send an ambulance too. Our suspect is injured. We haven't found the victim yet."

Jake saw the tire iron lying beside the man, and his hands balled up into fists. If he had touched Miranda! Jake wanted to punch the guy.

"Where is the woman you kidnapped?" Nick's brows drew together as he stared at the man.

"Don't know what you're talking about," The professor managed to mumble. "I'm the one who's hurt. Who cares about some woman?"

"On your feet." Nick dragged the man to his feet. It looked like the arm was broken so he didn't cuff him but started moving him toward the cabin.

Where's Miranda? Jake's mind screamed.

"You're under arrest for kidnapping. You may remain silent … " Jake heard Nick say; he noticed the professor remained silent, pressing his mouth in a straight line.

"Jake," Nick said.

"Yes?" He followed slowly behind the group.

"Call in SAR."

Jake grasped his phone and punched in the number. He gave detailed directions and then waited until the men had disappeared. He bent and whispered in Katie's ears as he unclipped the leash, "Go find Miranda."

CHAPTER TWENTY-FOUR

SATURDAY, OCTOBER 26TH

MORNING

Miranda's hands and knees felt like pincushions; thistles protruded from them and, every time she touched one, they seemed to embed deeper into her soft flesh. She'd need to pick them out somehow so at least the burning sensation could be alleviated. It seemed a daunting task. She held her hands palm-up and untied the strips of coat from her knees. She drew them up close to her chest as she sat on the fallen log. She had to start; the thistles wouldn't go away on their own.

She grasped one at a time. Like weeding a garden, pulling one out at a time with the root attached was better than grabbing a handful and leaving the roots, or in her case the barbs, under her skin. Without clear light, she had to carefully pinch the exposed section and tug steadily.

A cat yowled, and Miranda sat like a statue. Could the big cats smell her blood, and if so, what was she supposed to do? Should she get small or big, or scream to scare it away? She hunkered down in a crevice between the two fallen trees until she thought no part of her could be easily seen. What if it was the professor who caused the cat to yowl? No longer worried about all the stickers, she crammed herself further into the hole.

A low humming sound came from the dead tree. Uh oh, she'd disturbed something … but what? Something crawled up her legs, and she kicked and slapped at it, then felt something squish under her fingers. She could not lie here and be still! She had to get out of here! She bolted and shook her legs, slapping them to get rid of whatever bugs were attached. As an owl screeched and a coyote howled, Miranda jumped, and then crawled over the logs. She situated her body on a soft bed of ferns behind a tree. Her nerves were taut; remnants of crawling bugs tickled her skin; at the same time the burning increased where the barbs remained embedded.

Uneven footsteps penetrated the silence. Miranda covered her mouth to prevent any sound and held her breath. She saw flickers of light and clung to the tree. She didn't know how good the professor was at tracking, so she prayed. *Lord, keep him blinded to the path I took. You are my hiding place.* Miranda heard the limping step become a faint sound in the distance.

Slowly letting out her breath, she hugged her knees and leaned against the tree. Exhaustion was fighting to take over, she fought it but her eyelids closed and she couldn't make them open again. Sleep won out. Might this be her last thought? *Lord, I'm falling in love with Jake. Please bring him back to you.*

She batted away the wet slimy thing attacking her face. Her eyes flew open, and she shrieked. A yip sounded, and the black dog lay down. Miranda gawked. "Katie?" The name came out as a question.

The little dog jumped into Miranda's lap and started licking again. Miranda hugged the pup tightly, and suddenly the pup struggled free and ran away. Jake had come for her after all. He'd sent Katie to find her! Dread returned; the professor could be using Jake to find her. Miranda decided to stay still until she was positive the professor wasn't out there scheming.

Sunrays streamed through the tall evergreens. It was a morning like no other: she—was—alive.

Katie made three more appearances before Miranda heard the most precious voice. Jake was calling her name. Miranda tried to stand, but her joints were stiff from the cold and the crawling. She tried to call but could only croak out, "I'm here."

"Miranda, if you can hear me, stay where you are, and Katie will bring me to you."

She wasn't able to move anyway and her shoulder still throbbed. Jake was here and coming. She couldn't believe she'd been found. But … what if it was a trap?

Peeking around the tree, she saw her solid landscaper—and he was alone. Miranda waved and Jake ran, collapsing on the ground beside her. He examined her from head to foot, and she saw him cringe the second he saw the scratches on her face and the belt holding up her arm.

"Thank God you're here, Jake. I prayed, and he answered," she whispered. "The professor?"

"Miranda, Miranda. God answered my prayers too." He grasped her hands to look at her palms. His brows drew together as he spotted the barbs embedded. "You don't need to worry about the professor. Nick has him in custody. Nick called in the SAR team, but I couldn't wait for them. I sent Katie after you."

Miranda reached for him with her good arm and squeezed Jake's neck. "Jake, help me up and let's get out of here before you start to treat my scrapes and other injuries. I can make it with your help." Jake grasped her waist and carefully helped her to stand. She wobbled and almost tipped, but Jake's lightning-fast reflexes caught her and held her to his side. They started the trek to the cabin.

"Miranda what happened? And why didn't you wait for me inside your office?"

"Jake, you're right. I should have waited. But you're always on time, and with the threat of that note, I thought something happened to you. I left thinking I was safe with Doc. Oh no! Doc! Do you know anything about him? The professor left poisoned meat, and I saw him collapse." Miranda swallowed a lump, not wanting to cry.

"He's going to be fine. He will need to spend a few more days at the vet's office, though."

Miranda relaxed against him and looked down at her ripped, bloodstained coat. She knew her face with its scratches and lumps probably looked the same. "I look a fright." She lifted a hand to the left side of her head and felt a lump the size of a golf ball.

"No, you don't. You are more attractive to me now than ever before." He dropped a kiss on her forehead. "Tell me what happened."

She told him all that had happened, not leaving out any detail even when she saw his hands curl up into fists and his jaw clench. "I'm sure you would have protected me if you had been there, but isn't it great how God protected us both? I'm sure he was the one prompting me to move to the next hiding place. So—what did happen to the professor out there?"

"It seems he had an encounter with a porcupine and then must have lost his balance. He fell, and his arm landed in an old, rusty trap. It looked as though the thing had been there for years. But you are right about God." Jake's sheepish grin spread. "Hey, I haven't prayed this much since my parents split up."

Miranda's face glowed, and she gave him a beatific smile.

Katie kept running circles around them, then racing ahead and back. They continued making slow progress to the cabin, and before anyone could race up to greet them, Jake turned Miranda to face him, bringing his lips to hers. It was a sweet, protective kiss that promised a future. Her arm snaked around his neck, and she clung tightly to him.

As the cheers from the crowd erupted the two separated slightly and shared a private smile. Heat crept up to her face as she faced the crowd of SAR teams and police officers.

Nick was striding toward Jake looking thunderous. "Jake you can't disregard my orders like that. I'm responsible for your safety. I know we had the professor, but he does have a helper … one you have met. He was probably just someone paid to keep you out of the way for as long as possible."

"You're right. Do you know who he is?" Jake kicked the dirt and stared at it.

"We don't know. But you need to obey my orders for your own protection," Nick replied.

"I couldn't wait any longer. Miranda doesn't know how to survive out there, but I have to admit she seemed to take in some of the survival tips she heard," Jake defended and tightened his arm around her waist.

"Well, if there ever is a next time, you need to listen to me. Miranda, you need to go the hospital if what I see hurts as much as it looks like it does."

"Thanks," she said sarcastically. "I do hurt all over, but I think everything is just surface wounds."

"I'll go with her to the hospital," Jake offered.

"I don't think so. We need to get you back to your truck, and then you can meet her at the hospital."

Anne appeared next to Miranda. "Jake, I'll take over."

Jake reluctantly let Anne lead Miranda to the ambulance.

"Anne thanks. Can you come with me?" Miranda asked.

"Yes, my husband and son will take the dog home. We need to call your parents, too."

"I know, but I'd like to put that off just a little longer." Both ladies climbed in the ambulance and Jake jogged over to give Miranda one more kiss before waving them off.

THREE WEEKS LATER

They were back at the hospital, Miranda dragging Jake down the hallway to Valerie's room. Valerie had made a remarkable recovery from her head injury.

"Of course you'll be welcome," Miranda said. "And I'd like you to meet my parents. They already like you because of your part in my rescue."

Jake's face reddened under his beard.

"Did you come to the hospital the day you found me?" Miranda asked, an understanding starting to break through. "Did you meet my parents then?"

"No, I didn't, not exactly. I saw them coming out of your room, and then the woman I assumed was your mother made a comment about my long hair." Jake bent his head. "I didn't want to make trouble for you."

Miranda pivoted, held Jake's arms, and looked up into his face. She grinned and before long was laughing at the stricken look Jake gave her.

"Oh Jake, I'm sorry, but my mom can't seem to keep her mouth shut about the way things 'should be' or the way people 'should' wear their hair. She will be so embarrassed, and mark my words, she will apologize once she knows who you are to me. Come on and don't worry. Anyway, whose opinion counts more ... hers or mine?" Miranda continued to the elevator.

"Yours, definitely." Jake laughed.

"Good, because I'm the one you'll be spending most evenings with, watching movies and going out to dinner. No hiking for a while, though. Agreed?"

"Well, I was going to talk to you about that ..." he teased, and Miranda popped him in the arm.

It was quiet in the elevator on the way up, and Jake took a moment for a quick but possessive kiss. Miranda's eyes shone as she grabbed his hand and pulled him toward Valerie's room. When they arrived, it was full of chattering family and friends.

As Miranda had predicted, her mom stared at Jake. Her mouth dropped open, and she snapped it shut before whispering something to Betty Anne. With her arms outstretched, she bustled toward the couple and grasped Jake's hands.

"Jake, I can't apologize enough for the fool I made of myself the first time I saw you. Can you forgive an old woman and her unfounded prejudices?"

"Of course, I forgive you," Jake graciously answered.

Miranda pulled him away from her mother and whispered. "I told you so."

She then introduced him to her father and the rest of the gang. Her dad shook Jake's hand, and Betty Anne gave him a hug, but Frank, Val's stepfather, stood against the wall as though he had better places to be.

"Nick, I didn't know you were going to be here too." Miranda gave him a hug.

"Well, I'm reacquainting myself with an old high school crush—although she didn't know how I felt for her at the time. That's why I talked about Jesus so much to her." Nick winked at Val and she blushed.

"Good luck, man." Jake pounded Nick on the back.

Shuffling could be heard at the room's entrance. All conversation stopped, and everyone's eyes in turned that direction.

Miranda ran toward the newcomer and threw her arms around the tall, lanky young man, a man with a perpetual five o'clock shadow and whose short hair stuck out in all directions.

"Well, hello to you, too. Mom told me what happened, and I couldn't miss this gathering. I have a few weeks off. Now, please introduce me to the guy with the glowering face before he hits me," Robert said before laughing.

"Oh Jake, this is my brother Robert. I haven't seen him in almost a year," Miranda accused.

"Not my fault, I just haven't had any weekends off since Christmas. But the schedule's changing and I'll be making a pest of myself again."

Miranda moved back to Jake's side and clung to his hand.

Valerie spoke up. "Now that everyone is here, I'd like first of all to thank everyone for their part in my rescue. Miranda, Jake, and Nick. Miranda, could you tell Anne thanks, too?" Miranda nodded.

"I'm not good at speeches or apologies so I'll make this short and then answer any questions you might have," Valerie continued. "I've already told everything to my mom, and she can fill in some details." Valerie worried the sheet with her hands. "Mom, Dad, Mr. and Mrs. Jacobsen, I don't have the right words to express how remorseful I am for what I did with Jenny." Val's color heightened as she perused the faces bravely. "When Jenny and I took off, we were young and, yes, we pulled a stupid stunt. We didn't think of anyone but ourselves. We thought we knew everything and could show everyone we could live on our own."

Valerie took a breath before continuing. "But we were wrong. We hooked up with a couple of older guys who thought life was one party after another. At first, we had fun, but not long afterward we felt stuck but too embarrassed to try even to reconnect with you guys. And then we'd think about home, but remembered why we had left, and stayed where we were. In the end, we did learn that no matter where you live, or whatever situation you find yourself in, there will always be rules of some kind and consequences for behavior." Val looked to Nick, and he nodded.

"I decided to leave my boyfriend. By that time, Jenny and her boyfriend had already left that house, and I haven't been in touch with her since. My boyfriend was about to go into a drug rehab program, but unfortunately, he died before he started. So I took a job back in our hometown, not realizing Mom had moved. I did stay hidden from the Jacobsens, though." She faced them regretfully. "I couldn't tell them where Jenny was because I didn't know. So I avoided any contact and, well, God had other plans. Can you forgive me?"

"Of course," came a chorus of voices and everyone started talking at once.

Miranda twined her fingers with Jake's and they snuck out.

"Should we leave?" he asked.

"Oh, yes we should. We'll be back, but for now, I don't want to be in the hospital one minute longer. Let's get the dogs and go to the park." Jake grinned at her, and together, swinging their hooked arms, they fast-walked outside to get their dogs.

CONTACT INFORMATION

To order additional copies of this book, please visit
www.redemption-press.com.
Also available on Amazon.com and BarnesandNoble.com
Or by calling toll free 1-844-2REDEEM.

WEBSITE PAGE

It's been a long rewarding journey to finally finish this book. God has kept my focus on the path as he pulled me to the finish line. I have enjoyed seeing how Miranda and Jake's relationship has grown in this book. I've been through both the wondering if God is really there and hears my prayers and the knowing He is there and my strength during the times of trials.

Looking back on the writing of their story I see God's footprints and hope to see them as we continue Miranda and Jake's story along with meeting their family members and friends in the books to come.

Please feel free to visit my website.

www.donnabjorklund.com or www.miranda-rae-mysteries.com

CPSIA information can be obtained
at www.ICGtesting.com
Printed in the USA
FSOW01n0153071216
28021FS